SAVAGE fire

Savage Angels MC Series Book Two

Kathleen Kelly

Savage Fire
Savage Angels MC Series Book Two

Kathleen Kelly

This book is a work of fiction. Any references to real events, real people, and real places are used fictitiously. Other names, characters, places and incidents are products of the Author's imagination and any resemblance to persons, living or dead, actual events, organizations or places is entirely coincidental.

All rights are reserved. This book is intended for the purchaser of this book ONLY. No part of this book may be reproduced or transmitted in any form or by any means, graphic, electronic, or mechanical, including photocopying, recording, taping, or by any information storage retrieval system, without the express written permission of the Author. All songs, song titles and lyrics contained in this book are the property of the respective songwriters and copyright holders.

All efforts have been made to ensure the correct grammar and punctuation in the book. If you do find any errors, please e-mail Kathleen Kelly: kathleenkellyauthor@gmail.com Thank you.

Disclaimer: The material in this book contains graphic language and sexual content and is intended for mature audiences, ages 18 and older.

ISBN: 979-8401999047

Re-editing by Swish Design & Editing
Proofreading by Swish Design & Editing
Book design by Swish Design & Editing
Cover design by Clarise Tan at CT Cover Creations
Cover Image Copyright
First Edition 2015
Second Edition 2021
Copyright © 2021 Kathleen Kelly
All Rights Reserved

DEDICATION

To my wonderful husband, who puts up with me, Thank YOU. Your continued support always astounds me. When I am at my darkest hour, you always pull me back from the brink and remind me it's really not that bad. The night you told me I am your "Forever, ever love" healed all my old wounds, and, if possible, made me love you more. I look forward to our future together, 'cause, baby, it's only going to get brighter. (PS I still love you more.)

To Christina Olive Kelly, I miss you every day. Without you, I wouldn't have stories to tell. I think you would be proud of me, and I know you would be happy for me and the life I now have. I miss your voice and your hands, Mrs. Kelly, and all the other things that made you, you. You are remembered with much love and always with a smile.

SAVAGE *fire*

CHAPTER 1

EMILY REYNOLDS

I'm in the palliative care unit listening to my father take his last breaths. He smoked for many years and it's finally caught up with him. Cancer ravaged his body. I am amazed at how slowly the body can take in a breath as each one gets further and further apart. He's breathing through his mouth, so I occasionally place a swab in a mixture of water and lemon and rinse out his mouth.

The nurses say he doesn't have long to go.

I have a swab in his mouth when I realize he's no longer breathing. Bending down, I kiss his forehead.

"You could be a bastard, Dad, but I love you, and I hope you find Ma. I hope you find the happiness in the next life that you didn't find in this one."

Tears course down my face as I make my way to the nurses' station. It's three o'clock in the morning, and only two nurses are on at this time. No words are necessary.

The senior nurse pats my arm. "I'm sorry, honey." She picks up his chart. "We'll arrange everything. Go home and get some sleep. You've been here for a week, and I'm thinking it was only the two of you? Did you care for him at home, too?"

I nod as exhaustion takes hold of me, but I know sleep won't claim me. Too many things are running around in my head. My father and I didn't always have the best relationship. When my mother was alive, she kept him in line with his drinking, but that was five years ago. Dad's probably been sober for the last six months, and it's only because he was too sick to get out of bed, and there was no way I was going to supply it to him.

When my mother died, Dad went into depression and drank until he'd black out. He loved my mother in his own way. She was gunned down in a senseless robbery, and Dad couldn't move past it, but he tried.

He reached out to my older brother, Dane. They hadn't seen each other in over seventeen years, but Dane wouldn't even speak to him. My father pleaded with Dane, but Dane's response was always 'no.' He said he'd done his fair share of listening to Dad and wasn't about to give him any more time. Dane said he was sorry, but he'd made peace with those demons years ago.

As I walk through the hospital, my father's oncologist, Steve, stops me. "Emily, has your father passed?"

Steve's a good doctor, but he's made it more than obvious he'd like to date me. He's nice, but I haven't had a lot to do with the opposite sex, so I sort of fumble through our conversations. It's not as if I haven't had boyfriends. One was with a boy in high school, and we split up when we both went off to college. My second relationship was with a college boy, but we only dated for three months.

"Yes, just now." I stare at him, not really taking him in. I need to leave this place.

"Can I do anything for you?" His eyes are full of sympathy.

"What am I going to do now?"

"Come with me, Em. I'll get you a meal and something to drink." My gaze follows him, and he gives me a small smile. "You don't have any family left now, do you?"

"No, I have a brother." Memories of him come flooding back, and I remember Dane let me go through all of this alone. When he left us all those years ago, he walked out on me, too. He left me with an abusive father and a mother who always made excuses for him.

"A brother? Why isn't he here with you?"

I straighten my spine, square my shoulders, and say, "You're right! Why isn't he here with me? Why did I go through all of this alone?" My voice grows louder and more forceful.

"Em, you're in shock, sweetheart. Let me help you." His voice is soft, reassuring.

"No, Steve, thank you. Because of you, I now know what I need to do." I touch him on the arm as I walk past him, out of the hospital, and to my car.

Tourmaline is a four day drive from here. On autopilot, I climb into my car and begin the journey.

Dane has a lot to answer for.

CHAPTER 2

SALVATORE AGOSTINO
Captain in the Abruzzi Crime Family

Sitting in a chair, I watch, bored, as one of my men beats one of my crime family's competitors. The Abruzzi family promoted me to Captain, the youngest ever. The beating has been going on for far too long, and there's much I need to do. It's time for me to end it. Standing, I walk toward the bloody form, indicating for my enforcer to stop.

"Jerome, I need you to tell me who you're buying guns from. They're undercutting my business, and I can't have that." I smile at him and motion toward my man. "Jerome, he'll stop the beat-down if you tell me who it is."

Tony cracks his knuckles and sneers at Jerome with a sadistic gleam. He's only five foot eleven but built like a brick wall—sturdy and impossible to knock down—and when he hits someone, they stay down. Plus, he's loyal and has been with me from the beginning. When they made me a Captain, he was so proud of me.

Jerome mumbles something, so I crouch down over his body and study his face. "Jerome, you know it didn't have to be this way. Just give me the name, and I'll let you go. We'll be solid, give me the name."

His eyes find mine, well, the one which isn't swollen shut does. "Savage Angels, Tourmaline." It comes out as a croak. My eyes widen, and I shake my head. "I swear, I swear it! Savage Angels."

"Now, Jerome, I had a deal with someone in Tourmaline. The deal was they wouldn't undercut me or muscle in on Abruzzi family business. Who the fuck are the Savage Angels?" I grab him by the back of the head and lift him toward me.

"I swear. Please, Sal, please!" he pleads.

"Who. Are. They?" I pause between each word and shake his head.

"Savage Angels MC. They're tough motherfuckers, Sal, and they're everywhere."

I look him in the eyes and know he's telling me the truth. I stand, and Tony hands me a cloth for my hands.

"You want me to pound him a bit more, boss?" Tony looks down at Jerome as he tries to crawl away.

I smile at him and say, "I believe he's telling me the truth, Tony. Get him cleaned up and returned to his home. Make it clear to his family, there will be no retribution, and in the future, they will buy their guns from us. Yeah?"

"Yeah, boss, I can do it. Should I take one of the guys with me?" he asks.

I nod my head and say, "Take three, armed to the teeth, so if there are any problems, we'll have enough men and firepower to come out on top. Kill whoever you have to, to get our point across. Clear?" Walking toward the door, I stop, and place the cloth on a table and continue, "Don't kill Jerome. If there's a problem, kill his family."

Jerome groans on the floor, and Tony smiles and nods at me as I leave the room. When I enter the front of the warehouse, Guido is waiting for me.

Fuck.

He's the main enforcer for the Abruzzi family and works directly with the old man, Dominic. Obviously, they're concerned about business, but I can fucking handle it.

"Guido, how're things?" I smile and walk toward him with my arms open.

He envelops me in a quick hug. "Sal, same fucking shit, different day." We break apart, and he says, "Dominic sends his best."

Fuck, he's letting me know he is here on business. Instead of reacting to him, I say, "You must give Dominic my best. It's been too long since we've had a sit-down." I clap him on the shoulder, look down at his shoes, and play with my pinkie ring. Then I slowly lift my eyes to his.

"He's concerned about the Eastside. Business has dropped?" He makes it a question, but we both know, he already knows it has.

I smile and say, "I have it covered. Tell Dominic things will be back to normal, and since business has dropped, I'd be happy to make up the lost funds plus three percent."

"Eight percent, and he wants you to handle all of it yourself." He smiles, but it doesn't quite reach his eyes. I've fucked up big time, and if the family is sending Guido, I'm in over my head. Something bigger must be going on.

"Five percent, and we have a deal."

I hold out my hand to Guido, who smiles, grabs my hand, and says, "Seven."

I nod as we shake. "Seven, it is. I'll send Tony to fix this..." My voice trails off as Guido shakes his head.

"No, Salvatore, the old man wants you to fix this personally and... alone."

He holds my stare, and I raise my eyebrows at him. "Personally, and alone? Okay, Guido, what gives? I'm a Captain in this family, and I don't do errands." My voice is controlled, and my hands are at my side, but internally, I want to rip this fucker's face off.

"Only telling you what the old man said. He doesn't want those bikers stealing any more of our business. He wants it controlled, and he wants someone he trusts to do it, or he'll send me." The threat is clear. If he sends Guido, I'm as good as dead.

"Fine, I'll do it, and I'll go alone. Tell the old man I have it covered." I pause and look around the warehouse. "Perhaps, next time, if you find out who's undercutting us, you could possibly share the information, so it's handled more efficiently." My voice has gone icy, my intentions clear. I didn't get to be a Captain in this family by being a pushover. I'm deadly, and Guido knows this.

He holds up his hand in a placating manner. "Sal! You know how this family works, and you got the information, yes? So, it's all good! I'll tell the old man you have it covered, and you're paying him seven percent, then all will be good... so long as it gets fixed."

He holds out his hand again and smiles at me. Guido is Dominic's right-hand man. He's a cold-blooded killer, who only cares about one thing—money. He does the family's dirty work, and they trust him completely.

Grabbing his hand, I move into him. I'm slightly taller, so I look down at him. "Yes, Guido, tell the old man I'll fix it. Could you also tell him I don't like being threatened over my own business deals, and I did, indeed, have it... covered." My voice is steely, and my gaze says I'm not to be fucked with, but I'm playing a dangerous game as Guido is above me in the family and deserves respect.

He holds my gaze, then throws his head back in laughter. "Fucking balls of steel! I'll let the old man know. He wants it done fast. Here's my number, let me know when it's done." He has a business card in his other hand and holds it out.

Letting my hand go, I grab the card, and he heads for the door of the warehouse. He stops at the door, looks at me, shaking his head, then does a two-finger wave and is gone.

Fuck.

The fucking Savage Angels must be moving in on our other businesses. I stand in the warehouse for a moment, not moving. I rub my hand over my face, letting out a little frustration.

"Boss, you okay?" It's Tony, and he has sheer concern written all over his face. He knows the dangers of being in this family.

"Yeah, Tony, I'm good. Did you hear?" He nods at me. "I'll be going out of town for a while. Take care of operations here while I'm gone. You need help, you contact Carmine. Don't go to Guido, do you understand?"

"Yes, boss, I understand. What I don't understand is why you have to do this alone? Makes no sense. What if you get killed? You need protection, Sal. It's been a long time since you've been out on your own." Tony is a loyal soldier. I place my hand on his shoulder. He's right, it has been a long time since I've been out on my own, but I'm no pussy.

"I can still fucking look after myself, Tony, but you're right, it has been a long time. I can handle myself."

"Don't like the idea of you being out there alone. The Balotelli family has been making threats, and you'd be making it easy for them, going out on your own." He slips his hands into the pockets of his khaki, blood-splattered trousers. "I don't like this, Sal."

"The Balotelli thing is under control. I've negotiated a deal. It'll be fine. Now, what car do I take? Might as well get on the road." I take in a deep breath and hold it as I glance around the room. "Minimal bloodshed," I mutter as I let out the breath I was holding in a frustrated sigh.

"Take the Escalade, the black one. I have hidden gun compartments in it. You run into any problem, you'll have enough firepower to get yourself out." He doesn't sound happy, but he knows I have no choice.

"Thanks, Tony. I'll see you when I get back. I will call if there's a problem, okay?" He nods, and I head for the Escalade. I'm in for a long fucking drive.

CHAPTER 3

EMILY

I've been driving for three days. I haven't slept in over a week. I still have another day of driving before I get to Tourmaline. I have stopped along the way and picked up coffee and energy drinks to keep me awake, but it's my anger which keeps me going. Dane left me when I was eight years old. He was my everything. He was the closest thing I had to a father, and he left.

Suddenly, I have a pressing need to pee, so I pull into the nearest gas station and get out of my car. My whole body feels stiff and sore from the drive, and my movements are slow and clumsy. I stumble awkwardly into the store and head for the counter.

As I get there, a man steps in front of me and throws a bag of chips at the cashier. A gasp escapes me, but he doesn't turn around. "This, a bottle of water, and pump number three."

I shake my head at this man, but he doesn't even notice me. He's taller than me by about a foot. I'm five foot four and tiny compared to him. He pays the cashier and gives me a cursory glance as he goes back to his car.

I look at the cashier and shrug, and he smiles at me. "How can I help you, ma'am?"

"Could I please have the key to the toilets?" I ask.

"Here you go. They're out back. It's well lit, but be careful, yeah?" He smiles again and hands over the keys.

I roll my eyes. Great. It's well lit, but be careful? I tentatively make my way around to the bathroom. I don't see anyone, but I hurry in and lock the door behind me. I check the three stalls to make sure no one is lurking about. I take a deep breath—I'm safe. I do what I have to do, wash my hands, and make my way back to the front of the gas station. As soon as I round the corner, a man comes toward me. He grabs my arms and walks me backward toward the bathroom again.

"Now, blondie, I'm horny, and I don't have much time." He pushes me up against the wall and breathes into my face. His overpowering stench makes me gag. Stale beer and body odor invade my nostrils as he leans into me. "You can do this, one of two ways... a blow job or I'll fuck you from behind.

Your choice."

He pushes up against me, and I'm unable to move, unable to fight. I'm frozen in place, my legs threatening to give out.

A clearing of a throat interrupts my assault. "Excuse me. Which one of you has the toilet key?" I glance up, and it's the guy who so rudely pushed his way in front of me inside the store.

My attacker lets me go and steps away from me. I look at my savior, hand him the key, and run for my car. I'm in it with the door shut and locked in record time. I tear out of the gas station in a cloud of smoke and don't look back.

It's the last time I stop at night. I'm going to drive straight through to Tourmaline.

CHAPTER 4

SALVATORE

The female has run for her life and disappeared. What the fuck was she thinking coming back here by herself at night?

The trucker glares at me and says, "You scared my fun away, you fucker. I'll get you for that!"

"Go sleep it off. Real men don't force women." I lean into him. "You're lucky I'm feeling charitable. Otherwise, you'd find yourself sucking breakfast through a straw or in a shallow grave," I sneer. He backs down immediately, but his anger rolls off him in waves.

He wants to kick my ass. Bring it on, fucker, I dare you. He wouldn't stand a chance. I'd have my fist in his mouth and through the back of his head in a heartbeat.

"I was only going to play with her for a bit. Ten minutes, fifteen tops. Now, thanks to you, shithead, I'll have to use my hand."

I growl at him, and he backs away from me and heads for his rig. "Life's hard," I mutter. I keep him in my sights as he climbs into the cab of his eighteen wheeler, then I head for the toilets.

I walk back to the service counter and hand the key over to the cashier. He smiles at me and says, "Don't know what you did to the trucker, but he left you a present."

I look at him quizzically, and he motions toward my car. Son-of-a-motherfucker, the asshole has slashed my fucking tires! I now have two flat tires. *Fuck.* No good deed goes unpunished.

"How much for a new tire?" I growl at him.

"Two hundred and twenty dollars," he says with a smile.

I lean across the counter. "How much for a new tire?"

His smile falters, and he says, "One hundred and ninety-five dollars?"

I lean back, grab my wallet, and say, "I'll have two."

"Two?"

"Yes, two. I don't want to use my spare in case I get another flat. How much to put them on the rims?"

I pin him with my gaze, and he says, "I'll ask

Chuck to put them on for free. Won't take long."

Handing over my credit card, I continue to stare at the cashier. He processes my purchase, smiles at me, and says, "Thank you, sir, have a nice evening." I nod and walk out the front to wait for Chuck. I pull my cell phone from my pocket and check for messages, but there's nothing.

It's going to be a long night.

CHAPTER 5

EMILY

Lack of sleep is catching up with me. My mind is wandering, and I'm beginning to think, *what the hell am I doing?*

The road curves sharply in places as I head up into mountain territory. I reduce my speed, so I don't go over the edge as a vision of me crashing to my fiery death flashes through my mind and sends a shudder traveling down my spine. My mind moves back to Dane and what I'm going to say to him. I don't understand how he could have left us, left me.

As I drive, I get lost in my thoughts—thoughts of my father, my brother, my near assault, and how this will all turn out. I'm so deep in my thoughts, I nearly miss something dart in front of the car.

Swerving to miss it, I plow straight into a tree. The airbag deploys, and the windshield cracks. My arms go up to shield my face from the impact. Trembling in the seat, I'm stunned I can hear screams, and I realize it's me.

"Deep breath, Em, deep breath," I say to myself, trying to calm down.

I push the airbag out of the way and open the door. Slowly climbing out, making sure nothing is broken, I move to the front of my car. The hood is pushed up on one side. It's not going anywhere.

Goddammit!

Mentally, I kick my ass for not paying more attention. What the hell am I going to do now?

Headlights in the distance interrupt my ass-chewing. Thank you, Lord. I'm saved!

As the car approaches, I wave at it frantically. It pulls in behind my crumpled car. The headlights dim, but not before I'm momentarily blinded. Then, the driver's door opens, and a man emerges from the car.

"You." He sounds annoyed.

"I'm sorry?" My vision is still hindered, and I'm unable to focus on him.

"Does trouble follow you around, or are you prone to bad decisions?" He stalks toward me in a huff, forcing me to walk backward, and I collide with my car.

He stops in front of me, sighs, then his hand goes

to my face, and he turns my head from side to side. "Do you have a first-aid kit?" he asks.

"Yes, in the trunk. Why?" I feel startled at his touch and his obvious annoyance with me.

"You have a cut above your eye. Don't you feel it?"

My hand immediately goes to my face, and I feel wetness. I stare at my fingers covered in blood, and I feel dazed.

"Okay. Let's get you into my car. You must be in shock." His voice is authoritative. He has dark hair and nice, brown eyes. He puts one arm around me as the other grabs my hand and guides me toward his car. I'm overwhelmed by his masculine scent. When we reach his car, he leans me against it, opens up the rear passenger door, and produces a small first-aid kit. When he opens it, I notice a small handgun inside. I gasp, and his eyes move to mine.

"It's for protection, nothing else. I mean you no harm. My name is Salvatore Agostino. We met earlier tonight at the gas station. I saved you from the trucker."

He places the gun on the roof of the car, pulls out a gauze pad, and places it on my forehead.

"Thank you for saving me twice in one night." I try to smile, but tears form in my eyes. "I'm so tired. I haven't slept in days, and I don't know what the hell I am doing. I have no idea what I'm going to do now I've wrecked my car," I splutter through my sobs as tears course down my cheeks. Salvatore gives me a quizzical look as if he's waiting for me to continue. "What am I going to do?"

"Not only do you do foolish things in gas stations, but you drive without sleep. Do you have a death wish? Or are you hoping I'll be there to help you every time you get into trouble?" He smiles at me, and my legs buckle, but he catches me.

"Let's put you in the car before I have to lift you into it." Now he sounds amused as he opens the car door and helps me into it.

Once settled in the car, he says, "All right, amare, I'm going to check on your car, then I'll be right back. Do you think you'll be all right?"

"Amare?" I ask

"Yes, amare, as you haven't told me your name." Closing the door, he walks to my car. While I wait, I put on the seat belt and stare straight ahead.

I wake up when he opens the driver's door. "No, no, no, you can't fall asleep with a head injury." His tone tells me he's annoyed.

"I don't really have a head injury. The airbag must have grazed my face," I say.

"I hate to disagree with someone so pretty, but you have a cut above your eye, and it wasn't caused by an airbag. Stay. Awake." He hands me my car keys and handbag, then starts the car.

"Where are you headed?" I ask as I dab at the cut above my eye.

"Tourmaline. You?"

"Fate, it has to be fate." He glances at me. "I'm also headed to Tourmaline. I am going to visit my brother."

"Amare, you're putting blood on my seats. Why haven't you slept in days?" He turns on the interior light and flips down the passenger visor.

I look at my reflection in the mirror. He's right. I have a cut above my eye, and it's trickling blood down my face. I'm a mess.

"Hold the gauze to your cut, it will stop soon enough." His voice is gruff.

My mind feels like it can no longer process anything. I don't think it's from the accident, but from the man next to me. I glance at his profile—he has a strong jawline. Oh my goodness, his hands! They grip the steering wheel with such force, I wonder what they might feel like on me. I like his hands, they look strong and powerful.

"I'm so sorry. I'll pay to have your seats cleaned. Thank you, Mr. Agostino, for stopping. I'm not sure what I was going to do if you hadn't." My voice has gone soft, and my throat constricts with the tears which threaten to fall once more.

"Salvatore, amare, or Sal." He smiles at me. "Now, why haven't you slept in days, and why are you traveling alone?"

"My father died. I wanted to go to Tourmaline to tell my brother. I wanted to hurt him with it. Now, it all seems ridiculous. What was I thinking?" I share with Sal, but I'm talking more to myself.

"They don't have phones in Tourmaline?" he asks.

"What?"

"Phones, they don't have them?" He glances at me. When our eyes meet, the laughter bubbles up out of my throat, and I can't stop. Soon his laughter fills the car, making me more hysterical, then I sob. I know I'm making big gasping noises, but I don't seem to be able to stop.

I feel a hand in my hair as he strokes the back of my neck. "Shh, calm down. You're safe. You aren't badly hurt. We don't have long to go, maybe three or four hours, less if I speed. But I'd prefer to stick to the speed limit, amare. I think one car accident tonight is enough."

I nod frantically, and when I turn to look at him, I realize he's pulled the car over and is gazing at me. "Sorry, I'm good, I am good. Let's get going. I promise to stop, Sal, I promise."

"No, cry all you want. It's better to release it than to hold it in. The death of a father should be something to cry about. Not that I'd personally know, but I've been told."

He smiles at me as his hand massages the back of my neck. More tears fall down my cheeks, and I nod. He holds my gaze for a heartbeat, then nods at me, and we resume our journey to Tourmaline.

CHAPTER 6

SALVATORE

She makes quiet noises beside me, and I have no idea what words would comfort her. My father died by my own hands, and I was glad to do it. He was a rapist and a sadistic son of a bitch. He never cared for me, and I sure as hell never cared for him. This woman who appears so unprepared for this life as she blunders through it, almost getting herself killed—twice—has no place in my world. My enemies would eat her alive.

It's as if she has no sense of self preservation. She's lucky I was the one to find her both times, that I have a sense of honor and am not a rapist.

In the distance, I see a diner, and my stomach reminds me I'm hungry. "Are you hungry? Do you think you could eat something?"

I glance at her, and she nods. "I don't remember when I last ate. Food would be good." She smiles at me and then attempts to fix her appearance in the visor mirror.

I chuckle. "Amare, I don't think there will be anyone in there at this time of night to notice or care. Anyway, you're beautiful just as you are."

She goes silent and stops fussing. When I pull into the parking lot, I turn off the car and turn to look at her.

She stares at me with big doe eyes, and her mouth is slightly open.

Sighing, I say, "You shouldn't look at me like that. An innocent wouldn't fit into my life, nor would I want you to." As a blush creeps its way up her neck, she quickly looks away and opens the door.

Curious, surely, she knows how beautiful she is.

She stumbles through the door of the diner. I expected her to take a seat, but she waits for me. When I join her, she looks at me, and I motion for her to sit in the back, so I can face the front of the diner to see my enemies approach. Old habits die hard. I know there's no one out here who would hurt me or even try, but you can never be too careful.

A sleepy, old waitress approaches us. "What brings you young people out in the middle of the night?" Stopping in front of us, she looks from me to my companion and back again. Her eyes widen.

"I was in a car accident, and this kind gentleman stopped to help me. I hit my head." My companion stares at the woman and waves her hands around as she speaks. She'd make a good Italian—we gesture with our hands and talk all at once when we're in the same room together.

"Menus, do you have menus?" I ask as I stare at our waitress, who nods and walks away. "Why did you find it necessary to explain to the waitress?"

"To be polite. I must look a state. Can you see a restroom?"

I raise my chin and motion to the other side of the room. "Don't go outside, yes? Saving you twice in a night is enough." She half-heartedly smiles at me, stands up, and makes her way to the restroom.

The waitress comes back with some menus and behind her is a man, who I assume is the cook. He looks to be in his late fifties, heavyset, with salt and pepper hair. He's visibly uncomfortable as he shifts from foot to foot. As they come closer, I raise my eyebrows at him questioningly.

"Evening, Josie here mentioned the young lady might be in some trouble, and I should ask you about it."

"Trouble?" I ask in a mocking tone.

"Her face is all banged up, and she felt the need to explain very quickly. It's been my observation when a woman does that, she's covering for someone," says the waitress.

I sigh inwardly and think this woman is nothing but bad luck. Outwardly, I fix the waitress with a tight smile and try to explain the situation. "It happened like she said. I don't know her. I picked her up a few miles down the road. She had run into a tree and hit her head on the steering wheel." I stand, keeping my hands by my sides, palms up. "I don't harm women." I lean closer to the waitress and continue, "No matter their age or circumstance."

She takes two paces back.

"See, I told you, Josie, it was a misunderstanding." The cook smiles at me and says, "Of course, we'll need to confirm it with the lady."

It's been a long time since someone hasn't taken my word for something, and I'm about to explain to the cook that I am not a man to be fucked with when my amare comes back from the restroom.

"Is everything all right?" she asks, looking from me to the waitress to the cook. I can feel the tension building. I take a step toward her, but the waitress blocks my path. I pin her with my steely gaze, but she doesn't shy away. She outstretches her arms and moves into the space between us, trying to shield my traveling companion as though she can protect her from me.

The cook clears his throat. "Lady, we just need to hear what happened to you?" he says.

"Didn't Salvatore tell you?" she asks.

The old waitress turns her back on me and says, "We need to hear your side, honey."

I stare at the waitress blankly, in complete disbelief she would doubt my word. I shake my head and let out an exasperated breath. I've really had enough of this bullshit, and I'm ready to say 'fuck this' when I notice she's close to tears and her bottom lip trembles. I push past the waitress and embrace her, lightly stroking her hair so I don't scare her. I whisper in her ear in Italian, "Va tutto bene, amore, sei protetto, lo sei." *<It's all right, love, you are protected, you are safe.>*

The pull to protect her and take care of her washes over me. I tighten my hold on her, letting her know no harm will come to her.

"It's okay." She takes a shaky breath and begins her story. "I was in a car accident, but I shouldn't have been driving, I was so tired. Something... an animal... ran across the road, and I swerved to miss it. I hit a tree, and my airbag exploded. I was a mess. I'm blessed Salvatore came along when he did. He saved me." She pushes away from me and looks at the cook. "I'm not sure why you would doubt him. He really is my knight in shining armor."

The cook nods and walks away. The waitress stands there and looks at her for a moment, then she says, "Sweet or savory, sweetheart? What tempts you? We can do you both up a meal or get you pie?"

She smiles at the waitress and says, "Eggs over easy, toast, and pie to finish, please."

The waitress smiles and looks at me. "You, sir?" Her distrust of me has apparently vanished.

"I'll have the same, but I'd like bacon as well and coffee, lots of coffee." She nods at me, pats me on the arm, then heads for the kitchen, and yells out instructions to the cook.

I look at my companion, and the words she said to them are reverberating within me— blessed, knight in shining armor. No one has ever described me this way. Strong, feared, ruthless killer—these are the words used to describe me. I'm no one's safe haven, no one's salvation.

Her eyes lock with mine, and the air between us shifts quickly as she says, "Shall we sit? I'm so sorry I cried. It's embarrassing, really."

As she goes to move past me, I reach up and brush a tear off her cheek. "Don't be embarrassed. You're tired and overwhelmed with your situation. Once you've eaten, you'll feel better." We both turn and sit down.

"Relax, breathe," I tell her.

"You really are very kind."

Kind, there she goes again with complimentary words, words which don't describe the man I really am. "Thank you, but 'kind' isn't a word people use to describe me."

Her eyebrows pull together, confusion marking her features. "Really? Then how would you describe yourself, Salvatore? I've seen nothing but good from you."

I shoot her a smile. "That's a story for another day."

CHAPTER 7

EMILY

The waitress in the diner fell over herself to be nice to us. I have no idea why she thought Salvatore was a threat to me. I studied him over our meal. He really is handsome. His dark eyes penetrate my soul when he looks at me, and I can't help but tell him the truth. It feels as though he'd be able to tell if I was lying. He is gentle with me, but he's always in charge. When it came time to pay, he opened his wallet and pulled out a hundred-dollar bill and left it for the waitress. I tried to give him fifty dollars, even though leaving such a huge tip wasn't something I'd have normally done. He merely looked at me and waved his hand dismissively, then stood and held out his hand to help me to my feet.

"Come, amare, we can't be too far from

Tourmaline now. We should make it by daybreak." When I grab his hand, fire erupts, and electricity shoots through me straight to my core. He rubs his thumb over my knuckles and smiles. "Are you all right? You look... startled."

"I'm fine. I feel so much better. Thank you for stopping and getting something to eat, it's what I needed." I smile at him, trying to appear as though his touch hasn't affected me. He shoots me a wink and heads for the door, still grasping my hand.

As we arrive at the door, the waitress grabs my other hand. I turn to look at her, and she says, "Honey, you should freshen up before your drive. I couldn't help but hear you were on your way to Tourmaline. It's a bit of a hike. You really should use our restroom before you go." Her smile is sincere, and although I don't need to use the bathroom, I agree and let go of Salvatore's hand.

"I'll only be a minute. She's right, it's a bit of a drive, and this way we won't have to stop."

"Okay, fine. Go clean up. I'll be in the car." Salvatore nods at me and heads toward the car.

When I enter the restroom, I notice the waitress is hot on my tail. "Honey, he seems like a nice man, and he's very protective of you. Anyone can see it, but are you sure you're okay?" she asks.

"I've had a really long day. No, that's not right, it's been a long few weeks. It will be good to get to Tourmaline and sleep." I have no idea why I'm sharing this with her. Maybe it's her kind smile, or maybe it's because I haven't had contact with anyone other than the nurses and doctors who took care of my father.

"He looks at you like he either wants to protect you or devour you. Be careful of that one. Men like him will either break you or fill the void within. Good luck, honey." She pats my arm and moves out of the restroom.

I use the facilities and wash my hands. Staring at my reflection in the mirror, it appears as though I'm going to have a black eye. My blonde hair is a mess. I rummage through my bag, find a hair band, and rake my fingers through my locks to pull it up into a messy bun. Well, at least it's off my face. I sigh to myself and head for the car.

We hit the outskirts of Tourmaline as the sun comes up over the mountains. I've never been this far from my home, except for college.

Tourmaline is beautiful with its tree-lined streets and curving roads.

Salvatore has been fairly quiet since we left the diner. I'm drawn to him, but my inexperience with men means I don't know how to flirt or even make it known I am interested. The few times I have asked him a question, he has only responded with one or two-word answers. The guy is tense, on guard even, and seems lost in thought.

I study his profile and have the urge to run my fingers over his jaw. I know staring is rude, but this man who saved my life—twice—is worth admiring. I'm so taken by him, I don't realize he's speaking.

"What did you say?"

He laughs softly. "I asked where should I drop you off? A doctor? A motel? Your brother's?"

"Could you please drop me at the Savage Angels' compound? I think it's at the end of Main Street," I say.

His whole body tightens, and he glances at me and replies gruffly, "The Savage Angels' compound?"

I'm not sure why he has reacted this way, and I answer, "Yes, the Savage Angels' compound, it's on Main Street, and they have a garage there as well."

"Ahh, a garage for your car. Yes, of course, I can drop you there. Would you like me to come in with you?" he asks.

"No, thank you, you've really done enough already," I reply with a shy smile.

"When you aren't getting yourself into trouble, amare, you're a most pleasant companion." He smiles as he says this.

I grin at him. "Maybe I'm doing it on purpose, so you'll come to my rescue. It's not every day a girl gets saved by a handsome stranger."

He chuckles. "You think I'm handsome?" He stops the car and turns his eyes to mine.

I can feel the blush creep its way up my neck and into my cheeks. I immediately get flustered and stumble over my words. "It's just that... I meant it was nice of you to help me."

He nods and grins as he undoes his seat belt, then leans toward me and undoes mine. My whole body goes rigid as he gets closer, his mouth inches from mine. The warmth of his breath whispers across my face.

"You're at your destination." His fingers tuck my hair behind my ear as he reaches for the door handle, pushing it open. "Don't let them overcharge you for towing. Men will take advantage of women if they can." He hasn't moved from my space. We're in such close proximity, I think I've stopped breathing. His eyes search mine, and I think he's going to kiss me. My lips part slightly, ready to feel his mouth on mine, but the thought is quickly diminished when he says, "You can get out now, amare, I wish you well. I'm going to check into the local motel and sleep."

He turns away from me, facing back to the road, solely focused on getting away. I feel completely foolish. What the hell was I thinking. I mentally kick myself again.

"Thank you, Sal, I hope to see you again."

He gives me a quick lift of his chin and turns his eyes away again. Grabbing my bag, I climb out of the car and shut the door. I give him a small wave, he nods, and is gone. I feel like a complete idiot. Of course, he isn't interested in me. He told me as much at the diner. A man like him could have anyone he chooses, so why would he want me?

Even though it's early, I can see signs of life in the compound. I head through their gates and make my way to the office for the garage. As I cross the yard, a man comes up to me.

"Lady, you're too early for interviews and too late for the stripper job, so what can I do for you?" This guy is tall and covered in tattoos. He's only wearing a jacket, no shirt, putting his abs on full display.

"I'm looking for Dane Reynolds," I say.

He stops and gives me a once over. I feel like shrinking. "Dane's got an old lady, he doesn't need another one, and you, babe, well, it would be an injustice to have you as a side piece."

Shock goes across my face as I say, "I'm his sister, Emily."

He makes a clicking sound with his tongue and takes a step back, looks me up and down, then laughs sheepishly. He moves into my space and engulfs me in a hug, then pushes me back with his hands on my shoulders.

"I can see the family resemblance. I'm Jonas, Dane has mentioned you." He cocks his head to the side, studying me curiously. "You in trouble? Did some guy do that to you?"

I'm so not good with men. This handsome, rough-looking man, who's hardly dressed, has his hands on me, and again, I am overwhelmed. "No, no, no. I had a car accident and hit my head on the steering wheel. My car is a total write off... I think." I glance around, very unsure. "Is Dane here?"

His hands move to my face, and he presses around my eye. I wince a little at his touch. I try to focus on something else, his lips are moving, and he's talking. "Let's get you checked out by Doc Jordan. He'll be awake now, and then we'll give Dane a call, yeah?"

"It's really not necessary. I'm fine, really, just tired, and if you'd stop poking my face, I'm sure it wouldn't hurt as much," I snap as I pull away from his grasp.

He holds his hands up defensively and takes a step away from me. "Emily, Em?" I nod at him. "Em, we need to have you checked out. Dane would take off my left fucking nut if anything happened to you. So, in the interest of keeping my balls intact, would you please come with me to see the Doc?" He waggles his eyebrows at me, and I can't help but laugh.

"Okay, okay, even though I think it's a waste of time," I say. His smirk strengthens into a full blown smile as he motions for me to follow him.

"The Doc is only a block away. Think you can walk it?" he asks.

"Yes, but I really need to sleep."

"It's weird Dane isn't here to meet you. I'll call him."

I halt my steps, panic rising in my chest. "He doesn't know I'm here. I didn't tell him I was coming."

He cocks an eyebrow at me and says, "Dane told me your dad has been sick. Did he... pass?"

My throat constricts, and I continue walking. I nod repeatedly, but words will not form. I know if I speak, the tears which are threatening to fall will spill over, and I've had enough crying for now.

"I'm sorry, Em. I didn't mean to upset you. Tell me about your car accident and how you got here." He catches up with me, grabs me by the elbow, and guides me into a building.

"I swerved to miss an animal or something and drove straight into a tree. I didn't really think this trip out. I didn't even pack a bag. Dad... Dad died, and I've been existing in a haze for the last few days. I got in my car and began heading toward Tourmaline, toward Dane. I got picked up by a stranger who was traveling here as well. I got lucky."

Jonas looks at me, a blank expression on his face. "You've been driving for what, two or three days? Did you stop anywhere?"

"I've been driving nonstop for four days." I bow my head and sigh. I'm so tired. All I want is to sleep.

"Em, how far away is your car? I'll call one of the guys to pick it up." He reaches into his jacket and pulls out a phone.

"It's about four hours away from here."

He motions me to keep walking. "You didn't even pack a bag? Does anyone even know where you are? Do you know how dangerous that is?" He sounds genuinely concerned.

"I know. I didn't think it through. I had to see Dane." I don't admit to him I intended to hurt my brother, his friend. I wanted to wound him like I've been wounded.

"Jonas, I know your club donated a lot of money to my clinic, but it's a tad early to see patients, even for me." I turn to see a man, probably in his forties if I were to guess, striding our way. He has a close-cropped haircut and an enormous smile. His eyes are soft, despite the early hour of the day.

"Doc, I'm not trying to take advantage of you, but Dane's sister, Emily, had a car accident, and I'd appreciate it if you checked her out. Don't want the prez cutting my nuts off."

Doc Jordan comes closer to me and prods my face in much the same way Jonas did. I wince and take a step back.

"Sorry, Emily, it's probably only bruising, but let's check you over. If you'll follow me?" His tone is soothing as he makes a sweeping gesture with his arm.

I follow him into a smaller office and sit on the examination table. Jonas walks into the room too, and I raise my eyebrows at him. "Sorry, Em, I'll be gone in a minute, only a few questions, okay?"

I sigh, the weariness of my body seeping through me. Sleep, I need sleep. "Okay, what do you want to know?"

"Make, model, and color of your car, and what do you want me to tell Dane?"

I shake my head from side to side as fear rips through me. "No, don't tell Dane I'm here. I want to... surprise him." I feel bad for lying to Jonas, but I have no idea what I'm going to say to Dane. I intended to hurt him, but after traveling all this way, it seems ridiculous, childish.

He raises his eyebrows at me and smiles. "For now, I won't say anything, but, Em, babe, I don't like keeping surprises from my president."

I smile at him, and the doctor says, "Okay, Jonas, out. You can wait outside in the waiting room. This won't take long."

Jonas smiles at us both and retreats to the waiting room.

"Dr. Jordan, I'm fine, really," I try to reassure him

with a smile, but he frowns at me.

"Let me give you a quick look over and dress your wound. I don't think you need stitches, but maybe a little wound glue? Hmm... let's give it a good clean." He cleans my cut, and I wince. "Any headache, nausea?"

"I have a slight headache but no nausea. I'm tired." I think again about my lack of sleep and want to curl up into a ball.

Doc drops his hands to his sides. He cocks his head and looks at me intently. "Hmm... you look tired. When did you last sleep?"

He resumes cleaning my cut, and I say, "I haven't slept properly in a while. I was looking after my father. He had lung cancer. I couldn't sleep deeply since he may have needed me in the night. Every little noise would wake me." I try to smile, but I'm sure it looks more like a grimace.

Doc Jordan simply nods and continues to prod my face. I'm not good at silence. It makes me uneasy. I try for words to fill the void, but Doc beats me to it.

"It's not easy looking after a loved one when they come to the end. Some are good, some are bitter, and some want someone to blame. How was your father?" he asks.

"He was always a hard man, but he was so much worse at the end. He never lived in the now after my mother died, he only lived in the past. He was bitter, and he was..." My voice breaks as memories of my father flood my mind. Anger surges through me, and tears run down my cheeks. Doc Jordan walks over to his desk, grabs the tissue box, and hands it to me. He says nothing as he finishes cleaning my face and secures the cut with small butterfly bandages.

"There you go. Sorry if the antiseptic stung. You don't need stitches, and apart from the makings of a spectacular black eye and the fact you're exhausted, you appear to be fine." He pauses and looks me in the eyes. "I don't know the relationship you have with your brother, but he, too, is a hard man. He's the president of one of the largest MCs in the country. If you need anything, Emily, I can be found here." He smiles and holds out his hand to help me down.

"Thank you for patching me up. What do I owe you?"

He laughs and says, "Your brother made a sizable donation to my clinic, which will see me through for years to come, so it's on the house. Your family has a free pass for a very long time. Now, take these, they will help with your headache and help you sleep."

CHAPTER 8

JONAS
VP Savage Angels MC

I sit in the waiting room and patiently twiddle my thumbs. Waiting sucks, but I value my nuts. Emily needed a good look-over. She resembles her brother but is petite and very attractive with blonde hair, blue eyes, and a figure with small curves. Dane would rip my fucking nuts off and feed them to me if I made a move on his sister. She didn't tell me what type of car she has, so I can't send out the tow truck with the prospects until she comes out. It's strange she didn't tell Dane she was coming. I know he's fond of her.

I've known Dane for years. We both found the club at the same time. His story isn't all that different from my own, except I made peace with my family, and although we aren't close, we catch up for the holidays. Dane was never able to forgive his mother for taking his father's side. I can understand how he feels, but she was beaten for most of her adult life. She was never going to go against him. She wasn't strong enough. The sister, Emily, was born when Dane was only seven. I know he left when he turned fifteen. Although he didn't leave, his father threw him to the streets. Even then, his mother did nothing. I can't help but wonder if Emily is as weak as her mother was. We shall soon see.

I call Luke. He is a prospect and a good choice to get her car. "Luke, Jonas. Need you to bring the tow truck to Doc Jordan's."

"Jonas, what fucking time is it?" he sounds sleepy.

"Luke, it's fucking early, but get your ass here, yeah?"

"Okay, be there in ten." I end the call as Emily emerges from Doc's office. He has cleaned her up, but she looks pale and tired.

"So, how is she, Doc?" I ask.

"She's fine. I've given her something for the pain, but she really needs to sleep." He smiles at us both.

Emily offers him a weak smile. "I agree, sleep. Where's the nearest motel?"

"No, babe, you'll stay at the compound for now. I'm sure Dane will want you at his home but seeing as you want to surprise him... it's the compound."

"Oh, that's not necessary—"

I cut her off. "Trust me, it is. Anyway, it's a little early for Addy to have the motel open, and seeing as Dane isn't in town, you can have his room. It's clean, it's free, and you'll be safe." She looks from me to Doc, confusion crossing her features. "Emily, you're family to the MC. You don't know us, but we know of you." I look at Doc. "We good, Doc? You need anything?"

"There's something I need. The clinic I'm about to open in Pearl County needs a repaint. Could you spare a couple of men to do it? I'll supply the paint and feed 'em. What do you say?"

"Not a problem, Doc. When do you want them?"

"How about next week? Monday? Now, take this young lady home, so she can finally sleep." He pats Emily on the arm and walks toward the back of the clinic.

Doc is a good man. He's helped many of the poorer families in the area and not only for medical problems—he's found them new homes, cars, food, clothing, anything they need to live. Dane made a huge donation to his clinic, and it's helped more than a few people in this town.

Emily goes ahead of me and walks out of the clinic. Luke arrives as I hit the pavement. He's in the tow truck, his hair is wet, and he doesn't look happy.

"Jonas, what gives? It's too fucking early," he says, sliding out of the truck. He scowls at me as he approaches us, and I laugh.

"Luke, this is Emily Reynolds, and she had an accident out of town. We need to get her car," I say.

"Reynolds?" he asks.

"Yes, Luke, Emily Reynolds."

"Hello, pleased to meet you," she says as she holds out her hand to Luke.

He looks at her quizzically, then grasps her hand. "Likewise, so where's your car?"

"If you head back out of town..." she says as she points, "... and drive for about four hours, you'll find it. I impaled it on a tree. It's a silver Chevy Malibu." She smiles at him and hands him the keys.

"Four hours?" Luke has his hands on his hips and shakes his head in frustration. "Right. VP, I'll be gone for a while. Can I take Keg with me?"

Keg, another member of the MC, has been looking after Luke. Luke's girlfriend, Jess, was murdered, and Keg has been making sure Luke doesn't do anything which would get him killed or worse.

"Yeah, I'm sure Keg would fucking love climbing out of bed this early to spend time with you. If you can wake him, you can take him. Otherwise, pick another prospect. I don't care which one." Luke nods, does a two-finger wave at Emily, and then climbs into the tow truck. He'll make a good MC member one day. I don't think Dane is going to make him stay a prospect for long. Emily stands near me as we watch Luke drive away. She sighs and moves her eyes to mine.

"Whatever the Doc gave me is making me feel even sleepier if it's possible. I think I'll take you up on the offer of a bed." She tries to smile at me, but she looks exhausted.

"Come on, Em, let's find you a bed." She nods and walks toward the compound on unsteady feet. I grab her by the arm and put my other arm around her. She sure didn't inherit Dane's height—she can't be more than five foot two.

"Rebel!" I yell as I carry Emily through the doors of the clubhouse.

"Yeah, VP?" He walks out from the back of the clubhouse and wipes his hands on his jeans. He raises his eyebrows at me as I stride through to Dane's room.

"This is the Prez's sister, Emily. We've come from Doc Jordan's. She was in a car accident, and he's given her something for the pain. She collapsed on Main Street. I think she's exhausted. I don't want anyone going into Dane's room. You hear me? No one. I need you to make this happen."

He nods and pulls back the covers on the bed. I lay Emily on the sheets, take off her shoes, then cover her up. She's really a beauty. I push the hair off her face and turn to Rebel.

"Dane doesn't know she's here. Emily says she wants to surprise him, so keep everyone out and don't tell him. I'll be in the garage all day, but if she wakes, I want to know immediately, understood?"

He nods and says, "Yeah, VP, understood. Think Dane is still being kept prisoner by Kat, anyway." He smiles, but it doesn't quite reach his eyes. I think Rebel has an unhealthy crush on Kat, but you'd have to be blind not to see how much Kat adores our prez.

"Yeah, I'm supposed to be breaking him out tomorrow. Let's hope Emily is awake by then." I run my hand through my hair and head for the door.

Rebel follows me back out of the room and into the main room of the clubhouse, only to grab a chair and head back to Dane's room to stand guard, or in this case, sit guard, over our guest.

CHAPTER 9

SALVATORE

After I drop off my vulnerable companion, I drive to the local motel—The Country Inn. I wake the owner, an alcohol-soaked man in his late fifties. He's not happy about being awakened at such an early hour, but he soon changes his attitude when I pay him double for his troubles. The only highlight of my meeting with him is his very attractive daughter.

She explains the conditions of the rooms as she leads me to mine. "The rooms are clean, and if you need more towels or fresh linen, please come to the front desk and ask for me, Adelynn." She unlocks the door, turns her smile on me, and slips the key into my palm. "Remember, if you need anything, all you need do is ask."

"Thank you, Adelynn, I'm Sal. Tell me, do you happen to know where I can get a good meal around here?"

"There's a café on Main Street, Bettie's. She makes a fabulous apple pie, and you can walk to it from here."

"Thank you. Have you lived in Tourmaline long?" I ask.

"I was born here. But I've only been back for the last three years." She smiles and goes to leave.

"Would you care to join me for some breakfast?" I need information and having a meal with a beautiful woman is certainly a nice way to pass the time and hopefully glean something out of her.

"Oh, I can't, but thank you. My son needs some help getting ready for school," she says.

"I apologize. I didn't realize you were married," I say with my hands held up.

"I'm not anymore, my husband died a while ago." Before I can say anything, she continues, "Please don't apologize, it's been a long time. I came back to be with family. It's just me, my son, and my dad. But in Tourmaline, everyone knows everyone. It's a nice place to live."

"All right, perhaps another time?" I ask.

"Maybe. Enjoy your stay." She walks toward the main office, and I watch her go. She must be five foot ten, with long brown hair and a lithe figure. Her stride is deliberate and graceful, very pleasant to watch.

My room is more spacious than I thought it would be, and she's right, it's spotless. I walk into the bathroom, which smells of apples, and it too is clean and bright.

Taking off my jacket, I throw it on the bed. I need a shower and sleep, but before I can rest, I need information. I undress, place my clothes on the bed, and go into the bathroom. When I step into the running water of the shower, I find the source of the apple scent—the soap. I lather up and use it in my hair as well. The warm water washes over me, relaxing my muscles, but now isn't the time to forget why I'm here, so I turn off the heat and let the cold water wake me up. I need to be awake for my meeting with the Savage Angels.

I open the door to the diner and find a small group of people already seated inside. I plaster the best smile I can on my face and head for a seat at the counter. My hair is a bit of a mess as I don't have a comb or brush, so I run my hands through it. I'm sure I look like a well-dressed bum, but I smell nice.

The waitress watches me approach from the

other side of the counter and says, "What can I get you?" She's very young, maybe twenty. She has one of those boyish shapes—no chest and no ass. Her hair is pulled up neatly in a ponytail. Her name tag tells me her name is Rosie.

"Morning. A coffee, eggs over easy, bacon, toast, and pancakes." I smile at her, and she smiles back.

"Well, I sure like a man who knows what he wants," she answers flirtatiously. "You want maple syrup on those pancakes?" she asks.

"Yes, please, and I take my coffee black, no sugar."

"All righty, then, I'll go rustle up some coffee, and I'll ask Howie to get started on your order." Another innocent smile flits across her face, and I respond by offering some of my hidden charm. This one will be easier to retrieve information from, especially if she thinks I like her.

She grabs a mug, pours coffee into it, and places it in front of me. "So, what brings you to Tourmaline?"

"I'm here to visit an old friend. Perhaps you know her, Christina Saunders?"

Her face clouds over, and she looks upset. "I'm sorry to tell you this, but Ms. Saunders died a while back. It's been over a year."

"I didn't know," I say, lowering my eyes to the mug in front of me. "I was coming to town to discuss some business with her. Do you know who's looking after her transport business?" I do my best to look upset. I knew Ms. Saunders had passed. I was notified, of course. She was a major player in the gun business, but she knew better than to sell on the East Coast. The Savage Angels are about to find out you don't fuck with the Abruzzi family.

"I'm so sorry. She was a nice old lady. Her business is now in the hands of the Savage Angels. They have a clubhouse at the end of this street."

Before she can say anything else, the cook, Howie, yells out, "Rosie! Order up!" She rolls her eyes and goes to fetch my breakfast.

It's a little after ten as I make my way toward the Savage Angels' compound. It really is a pretty little town, and my breakfast was surprisingly good. Rosie knew little about Ms. Saunders. All she kept saying was what a nice old lady she was. Ms. Saunders was anything but nice. I only had a sit-down with her once, and she made it clear she wouldn't interfere with our business on the East Coast. On the odd occasion she breached her word, she gave us a healthy percentage to appease the family. She knew how things worked. She was a crafty old woman who would slit your throat while smiling at you. She looked like your grandmother, and people always underestimated her. I did not. Her reputation preceded her, as did mine.

It was about six years ago, and she came to New Jersey for the sit-down. I wasn't a Captain back then. I was a soldier trying to get noticed. She walked into the room and looked around at all of us, then sat at the table with the head of our family, Dominic Abruzzi.

> *"Dominic, my friend, how are you?" she asked.*
>
> *"Christina, it's been a while. I was told you had retired."*
>
> *"It didn't sit well with me, Dominic. I need to keep busy." She smiled and turned her eyes to me. "I see you have some new faces since I was here last."*
>
> *Dominic looked at me and motioned me to come forward. "This is Salvatore Agostino. He's been making a name for himself. He's proving to be a good soldier."*
>
> *"A soldier? Is that what you are, Salvatore, a soldier? Or do you long for more?"*
>
> *"I serve at Don Dominic's leisure, and I hope I do it well. I hope all my efforts will be rewarded one day, but it's up to him," I said.*
>
> *She laughed and looked around the room. "Dom, if you don't promote this one, you'll lose*

him. He's ruthless and will do anything to get what he wants. I know. Some of my other businesses have been affected because of this one."

"I serve the Don. Do not undermine my allegiance to him," I growled at her.

"Now, Salvatore, I didn't mean to insinuate you aren't loyal, merely ambitious."

"Christina, I need some assurances you won't be tampering with my business deals here on the East Coast," the Don said.

"No, Dom, I wouldn't interfere with any of your deals. I'll keep to the West Coast. If anything overlaps, I will pay our usual sum. Yes?" she asked.

"It's been a while, Christina. I'll be needing a little more if we... overlap." He smiled at her, but it didn't reach his eyes.

"Of course, Dom, of course! Forgive me. It's been a while, say plus ten percent?"

"Now, Christina, say fifteen percent, and we have a deal."

"Fifteen on top of what I will already pay you?" She looked at the ground, then raised her eyes to his.

"Twelve."

"Agreed! Now, my wife has made you some cannoli. It's divine. Let's have coffee, too." He got up and walked away.

She looked at me and said, "He's slipping, he should've asked for more. But you know that, don't you, Sal?"

"It isn't up to me to question the boss," I said.

"If he doesn't promote you soon, you come see me. I can always use a man like you."

"I am a part of the Abruzzi family. Your business could not compare." I laughed at her.

Her eyes never left me, and she didn't laugh. "Oh, Sal, you disappoint me. Who do you think stopped the deal with the Balotelli family? I have my fingers in more than a few pies."

"You stopped the deal? How?" I asked.

"The head of the Balotelli family owed me. You know how this game is played. One hand greases another. Perhaps one day we could be of use to each other."

After that, we occasionally spoke on the phone. She kept her word and stayed away from our business on the East Coast, and I can't be sure, but I believe she had a hand in my early promotion. To what end, I don't know.

As I walk across the Savage Angels' compound, I take in how many men are in the garage and who's out the front. Call me cautious, but it's kept me alive this long. I push open the doors and walk up to the bar.

"Little early for drinks, isn't it, buddy?" A rough-looking man appears behind the bar.

"Yes, I suppose it is. I'm here for information." I

smile at him, and he leans forward, putting both hands on the bar. "I was in at Bettie's Café, and Rosie said old Ms. Saunders had passed and the Savage Angels had taken over her business. I've had dealings with Christina over the years and hoped to continue the relationship." I offer him a reassuring smile, but he does not smile back.

"It's not the Savage Angels who inherited Ms. Saunders' business. It went to our president, Dane Reynolds." He stops and takes me in. "He employs us to take care of the runs and work at the depot. What kind of business did you say you were in with Ms. Saunders, Mr.?" he asks.

"Thank you. You've been most helpful." I turn to leave, and four men stand in and around the doorway. I hesitate for a moment, then walk past them and out into the fresh air. No one tries to stop me, and this confuses me. As I walk back to The Country Inn, I feel the hairs on the back of my neck bristle, so I know I'm being followed. I have no problem with that, the sooner I have a sit-down with Dane Reynolds, the sooner I can clear this mess up and go home. For now, I need to sleep.

When I arrive back at the motel, I go to my car and grab the gun Tony has left for me taped to the underside of the driver's seat. I'm sure, knowing Tony, there are more guns hidden throughout. We have been together for a long time, so if I need them, I'll be able to find them.

I enter my room, pull the curtains, and position a chair underneath the handle of the door for a little bit of added security. Then I strip and take another shower, letting the warm water flow over me and ease my tired muscles. Before I let sleep claim me, I place the gun under a pillow on the bed and turn the air-conditioning down to sixty degrees. I find I always sleep better in the cold. I lay there for another few minutes, listening to the sounds outside, and then allow myself to sleep.

CHAPTER 10

EMILY

I wake up, momentarily confused as to where I am before it all comes flooding back to me. Rolling over, I groan, remembering the events leading up to me being here. Jonas must have carried me the rest of the way. I sit up slowly. The throbbing in my head reverberates through my ears, and for a moment, I think my head is going to explode. I throw my feet over the side of the bed and stand on shaky legs. Walking across the room, I open the door and find a man sitting directly in front of the door. He slowly moves his head in my direction, and when he looks at me, a smile spreads across his hard features. He stands, his hands up in a non-threatening manner.

"I'm Rebel, Emily. Jonas carried you in here from Doc Jordan's. Do you remember?" he asks.

"Yes, is Jonas here?" I poke my head out the door and see a group of men staring back at me from the main part of the clubhouse.

"No, he's at the garage, but I can get him, if you want?"

I look at him and say, "No, it's okay. I can go find him." I move my hand to my head and wince. My headache feels much worse.

"You got a headache?" I nod at him, but it makes my head hurt, and I wince again.

"You've been asleep for a day. You're probably dehydrated, and you haven't eaten. I'll find you food, water, and Advil. Wait here, okay?" He gives a slight nod and moves out into the hallway. I walk back to the bed and sit down, resting my hands on the comforter. It's as though I'm moving in slow-motion when my head lolls off my shoulder. I realize, in the quiet of the room, I haven't showered in days. *So hot,* Emily, I scold myself. You probably smell awful. I need new clothes and a shower.

"Here you go. I've asked one of the prospects, Luke, to go get you something to eat."

He passes me the bottles of Advil and water, which I gratefully accept. "Thank you. Is there anywhere I can shower?"

He points to a door on the other side of the room and says, "Through there. This is the President's room, so he gets the ensuite." He grins at me and continues, "We couldn't find any clothes in your car.

Maybe they were taken?" he asks, eyebrows raised.

"No, it was kind of an impromptu visit, and I didn't pack anything. Luke, he's the guy I met with Jonas, he got my car?" I asked.

"Yeah, you've been out a long time. He's a good guy. He said your car is in a bad way."

I drink the water down and take two Advil. The cool water feels good going down my throat. Rebel's right, I'm dehydrated.

"I hit a tree. Do you think they can fix it?" I ask.

"I haven't seen it myself. I was on guard duty. If they can't fix it, I'm sure Dane will work something out."

"Guard duty?" I ask.

"Yeah, Jonas wanted you kept safe. I'm the one he volunteered to watch over you." He smiles at me, and I nod.

"Sorry, Rebel, you must be tired, too."

He smiles at me and runs a hand over his shaved head. "Well, I could use some shut-eye and a shower, too. But it's okay, I don't mind." The whole time I'm talking to him, I'm sipping the water and don't realize there's not a drop left. He points at the empty bottle and says, "There's more where that came from. I'll get you another. Why don't you go shower?"

"Thank you. I think a shower might help clear my head," I say, and he walks out of the room, pulling the door shut.

The shower feels fantastic, and it feels so good to be clean. I stand under the water and think about my decision to come here. If my car was fixed, I think I'd leave and go back home. I sigh and turn the water off. Stepping out of the shower, I towel myself off, and glimpse my reflection in the mirror. I hardly recognize myself. My eye is a lovely shade of black, but the cut above seems to be healing nicely. I'm still a complete mess, though. I look around the bathroom. Thankfully, there are toiletries available, along with a brush and comb. Thank goodness for a woman's touch.

I'm standing in the middle of Dane's room in a towel when there's a knock at the door.

"Yes?" I acknowledge.

Jonas walks in and stops dead in his tracks, staring wide-eyed at me. "Sorry, but I didn't want to put my clothes back on. I've been wearing them for days."

His eyes drift over my towel-clad body. "Kat has some clothes here. She's a little taller than you, but they should fit. I'll be in the bar, come find me when you are..." he takes in my body again, "... dressed."

I rummage through the dresser and closet and eventually find a nice dress, but all of Kat's bras are way too big for me. I don't like not wearing one, but I'm small-chested, so it's not much of a big deal. I slip on my shoes and make my way toward the bar area.

Jonas waits there with Rebel. There's another half-dozen men sitting around, and everyone's eyes are on me. I feel so self-conscious. One of the men sitting on a stool stands up and walks toward me. He's huge in every way possible—height, weight, and even his beard is massive. He smiles at me, and when he's within arm's reach, he engulfs me in a hug. All the air leaves my lungs in a whoosh, and a little squeal escapes me.

He holds me at arm's length. "I'm Bear, Road Captain of the Savage Angels, and you look just like your brother!"

He engulfs me again, and I hear Jonas say in a quiet, even tone, "Bear, enough. Can't you see she's terrified, and you're squeezing the life out of her?"

"Terrified? Of what? She's family!" he roars at Jonas and places one of his big arms around my shoulders. "Now, Emily, what were you thinking driving all this way? We could have picked you up, or you could've gotten a plane or train. Seriously, woman! Dane is going to be so happy to see you!"

He's nothing like I imagined a member of the Savage Angels to be. He's happy and jovial. I expected them to be more serious and dangerous.

"Don't mind Bear, Em, he's harmless. Do you want us to take you out to Dane's now?" says Jonas.

"I have one thing I need to do first, if that's okay?" I ask. His eyes flick to Rebel, then to Bear. He does not appear happy with my answer. "I would like to thank Doc Jordan and the man who brought me here. I'm not sure how long he's staying. He could be gone already."

He nods and sighs. "I have to go out to Dane's now." He looks at Rebel. "Reb, you'll keep an eye on Em, yeah?"

"It's not necessary. I've been on my own for a long time and in a city. Tourmaline should be a walk in the park. I'll come back here when I'm done. Anyway, Rebel could use the sleep." I lock eyes with Jonas as he appears to be weighing me up.

Eventually, he gives in to my request. "Okay, Em. You come back here when you're done, and one of the boys will take you out to Dane's place."

"Thank you." I look up at Bear, who lets me go, and head for the beautiful day outside.

"Em," Jonas says, "You run into any trouble, you tell people you're Dane Reynolds' sister, and they'll leave you be."

"Trouble?" I shake my head at him. "What kind of trouble can you get into here?" I go to leave but stop and turn around. "Rebel, thank you for keeping watch." He nods, a hint of a smile in his eyes, and I continue on my way out of the compound.

I head straight for Doc Jordan's. When I enter the room, there's a middle-aged woman behind the waiting room desk, and she looks a little frazzled.

"Hello, is Doc Jordan available?" I ask.

"The Doctor is with a patient. Do you have an

appointment?" From the way she has asked me the question, she knows I don't.

"No, I don't need an appointment. I only wanted to thank Doc for fixing me up. Could you tell me when he's available?"

She huffs at me and looks down at a calendar. "He'll have a spare minute in about an hour."

"Thank you, I'll come back then." Giving her my best smile, she huffs at me again and looks back down at her calendar.

I walk back out onto the sidewalk and see a café called Bettie's, so I head for it. It's early in the morning, but it's open. When I push open the door and enter, the place is bustling with people. The food must be good.

The waitress behind the counter gives me a huge smile and says, "Welcome to Bettie's! What can I get you?"

Everyone in the café turns to stare at me. I feel very self-conscious, especially with my black eye. At least I've tamed my hair into a ponytail.

"Good morning, could I please have a white coffee and a black coffee to go?"

She nods at me enthusiastically. "Is that all, honey? No food? We make great waffles and bacon." Her smile is infectious, and it's hard for me to say no.

"I'll come back for breakfast. I wanted to give someone a coffee as a thank you," I say and smile back at her.

She gives me a slight nod and fills up two cups. "Bring them back here. I'm sure once they've tasted it, they'll know it's the best coffee in the county."

"Thank you, I'll try." I smile at her and pay for my order.

The rest of the patrons continue to stare at me. I smile at a few of them, then make my way back outside.

The motel isn't far up Main Street. It doesn't take long to get anywhere in this town, and before I know it, I'm at the motel.

I can hear voices in the office, and I open the door. There's a man on the floor, and he groans as a woman tries to pull him to his feet. From the doorway, I can smell the sickly stench of alcohol—a scent I know all too well.

"Dad, I need you to stand up. We have a busload of people coming in, and I need to get Ben to school. Please, Dad!" She doesn't notice me until I clear my voice. "I'm so sorry, but we don't have any vacancies." Her face is one of pain and embarrassment.

I put the coffees down on the desk and walk around, standing next to her. "How about I help you with him? My name is Emily. You haven't got a hope of getting him to his feet on your own. Trust me, I know."

She holds my gaze for a moment, then sticks out

her hand. "My name is Adelynn. I could really use the help. I didn't want to ask anyone. You know how a small town can be. He's not always like this. He's my father." Her eyes go to the man on the floor, and she looks sad.

"Adelynn, I'm not from here, and I won't tell anyone. My dad was like this, too. I know you said he's not always like this, but I bet he drinks all the time. I can also guess he's not so nice most of the time, too. My dad was abusive. He died recently from lung cancer, but before he got sick... hell, his whole life, he was a miserable bastard." My eyes fill with tears as I stare at the drunken man on the floor and remember all the things my father did to me. There was no one else to look after him.

What was I supposed to do, abandon him like Dane did?

Adelynn puts her hand on my arm and I look at her. "I don't know what to do. I throw out all the bottles, and..."

"And he buys new ones, or he asks someone to buy it for him. He promises to be better, and for a while he is, then..."

"Then he goes back to this," Adelynn says as we both stare at the man on the floor. He's wet himself and snores. I let out a sigh, bend down, and grab one of his arms while Adelynn does the same. We lock eyes, and we both pull on his arms until he's in a sitting position.

He wakes and stares at Adelynn. "I'm shorry, Addy. Jusht had a couple." His words come out all slurred as he tries to get his feet under him.

"It's okay, Dad. I'm going to pull on three, and you're going to stand up, okay?" He nods at her, but you can tell he's barely awake. She looks at me, nods, and says, "Okay, Dad... one, two, three!"

We both pull as hard as we can until he's on his feet, an arm flung over each of our shoulders. He's much taller than me, so it's a little more difficult for me to maneuver him. It's obvious Adelynn has had plenty of practice. She guides us through a doorway, down a short hall, and we enter a bedroom.

"Do you think you could hold him up against the wall while I run and fetch some towels?" she asks.

"Yes, go, I can handle him for a second." She gives me a tentative smile and dashes out of the room. I have both my hands on his chest as he leans against the wall. He's so drunk, he falls asleep standing up. I'm grateful his legs haven't given out on him. When Adelynn returns with two towels, she pulls the covers back on the bed and lays them on top of the sheets. Then, together, we manage to put him on the bed.

Without looking at me, she says, "Thank you, Emily, you can go now. I appreciate all your help." I nod and walk out of the room.

There's no way I'm leaving her to clean up her

father's mess alone. I leave the office in search of cleaning supplies. Finding a mop and a bucket, I fill the bucket with hot water and return to the office to tidy up. When I finish, I empty the water from the bucket, refill it with disinfectant, and go back to sanitize the office. Adelynn returns as I'm emptying the bucket for the second time.

"You didn't have to do that," she says.

"Yes, I did. It would've been nice if just once someone had done this for me. I know the shame, the embarrassment, the anger you feel, and then you have to clean up after them. It's not fair to you or him. You need to do something, Adelynn, to make him stop for good. Otherwise, this will be your life forever, and trust me, you don't want that."

I think of my now cold coffees and head for the door. I stop and turn around before leaving. "I don't know how long I'm going to be in town for. I totaled my car." I point to my face and smile. "I did a good job. But if you want to talk or want some help, all you have to do is ask, okay?"

She straightens her spine, walks toward me, and embraces me in a hug. "Thank you." Pulling away, she looks down at me. "What made you come into the motel?"

I take a step back from her and grab the coffees. "A friend is staying here, and I thought I'd bring him a coffee. His name is Salvatore Agostino. I was coming in here to ask for his room number."

She smiles at me. "He's in room five."

"Thank you," I say, smiling back at her.

"Your coffee is going to be cold by now. How about you come in the back, and I can refill it for you?" she says.

"That would be wonderful! Thank you, Adelynn. Lead the way!" She laughs and heads back into the hallway, and I follow.

CHAPTER 11

SALVATORE

I'm headed to the motel office in search of fresh towels when I overhear the conversation between Adelynn and my amare.

"You didn't have to do that," Adelynn says.
"... Otherwise, this will be your life forever, and trust me, you don't want that." The compassion in her voice is endearing. It's obvious she's endured the same trauma. There's a pause in the conversation, and I'm about to knock on the door when my amare continues, *"I don't know how long I am going to be in town for. I totaled my car. I did a good job. But if you want to talk or want some help, all you have to do is ask, okay?"*

"Thank you. What made you come into the motel?"

"A friend is staying here, and I thought I'd bring him a coffee. His name is Salvatore Agostino. I was coming in here to ask for his room number." After all she's been through, she went and got me coffee. This woman is amazing.

"He's in room five," Adelynn says.

"Thank you."

"Your coffee is going to be cold by now. How about you come in the back, and I can refill it for you?" I can hear the smile in Adelynn's voice.

"That would be wonderful! Thank you, Adelynn. Lead the way!" I hear my amare laugh, as she moves further away from me.

I stand in shocked silence for a moment and then head back to my room. There's more to my amare than I thought—a hidden strength I didn't think she possessed. From the little I had to do with the motel owner yesterday, I could tell he was soaked with alcohol, so I can only guess they were talking about him. The woman I rescued, twice in one day, didn't appear to have the capability of looking after herself, let alone an alcoholic.

Her kind words to the woman, Adelynn, move me. Shame, embarrassment, and anger, these are all words I understand. My father made me feel this way, not because he was an alcoholic, but because he was sadistic and ruthless. My mother put up with him for years. He cheated, lied, and eventually used her like a punching bag. Then he'd use her body any way he wanted. Eventually, he tired of her and moved on, but my mother never recovered. The men she chose after my father were carbon copies who only wanted her for what she could give them. I could never make her see the light. I couldn't save her, I tried. In the end, I had to walk away and hope she'd save herself, but she never did.

Back in my room, I remove my jacket and shirt, then sit on the end of the bed and anticipate my amare's arrival.

CHAPTER 12

EMILY

I chatted with Adelynn for a while and discovered her mother died of cancer a while back. She told me she was married to a wonderful man named Ricky, and he was killed six years ago in Iraq. He was in logistics and supply and was killed by an IED when it blew up and destroyed the truck he was in. They have a son, Ben, and he's eight. He doesn't remember his father. Adelynn moved back to Tourmaline after Ricky's death to be with family and help her father. She didn't realize he needed more help than she's capable of giving.

After our chat, I head toward room five. My stomach is in knots, as I don't know what kind of reception to expect. I knock on the door, and Salvatore answers, stepping out and into my space.

He has no shirt on, and goodness me, does he look divine. I notice the tattoos across his chest and down one arm. I've never seen such a well-sculpted physique. I have a fleeting thought of running my lips over his skin.

For a moment, I'm speechless, but he breaks me out of my thoughts when he says, "Amare, what brings you to me again?" His voice is deep and gravelly. I slowly drag my eyes to his, and when I do, he has a knowing smirk on his face.

"I got you some coffee... to say thank you and..." I pause and stare at his chest again and say, "... I thought maybe I could buy you breakfast. The café apparently makes amazing waffles..." I slowly raise my eyes to his and find he's still wearing a knowing smile.

He puts his arm around me and ushers me into his room. "Come in, while I put a shirt on." He closes the door, and I stand there like a mannequin, searching my mind for something amusing to say. I'm barely inside the room, my back almost up against the door. He bends over the bed, grabs his shirt, and faces me. Again, he comes into my space and touches both my hands. "So, which one is mine." I hold up my right hand slowly, but he takes both cups out of my hands and places them on a small table. Then he returns to me, and I find myself pushed up against the door as he examines my face. "Ahh, I see you've had this treated." He has his body pressed up against mine as his hands prod my face. "I don't think you'll even have a scar. Tell me, did they tow your car to the compound?"

I'm completely overwhelmed. My core is on fire, and I want so much to touch him, to kiss him. I feel sparks of electricity shoot through every fiber and nerve ending in my body, screaming for release. I want his hands on me, all over me.

"Amare?"

I put my hands on his chest and push him away. He's too close, making it hard to form a single thought. I take two steps to the side to put some distance between us, so I can speak like a human, not a lust-induced zombie. "Yes, they towed my car, and it's in their lot. I haven't really spoken to them about it yet. I kind of fell asleep on them..."

His face clouds over. "You kind of fell asleep on them? What. Does. That. Mean?" He pauses between each word and growls them at me.

"Jonas took me to see Doc Jordan, and he gave me something for the pain, but because I hadn't slept in days, it made me sleepy. I think he ended up carrying me to their clubhouse." I realize how all this must sound. If someone told me the same story, I'd be thinking the worst.

"Did they touch you?" he growls at me, his eyes blazing with anger.

"No, no, no! In fact, Jonas put a guard on my door so no one would go near me. Not that they would. I was safe, Sal." Something crosses his face, and he stares at me so intently, it forces me to look away and stare at the floor.

He moves back into my space and tilts my head back. "Thank you for getting me coffee. Let's go have breakfast, and I'm buying. I think I shall keep you in my sights to make sure nothing else happens to you. I have never met a woman who allows herself to get into so many dangerous situations in such a brief space in time. You, my amare, are a handful." He moves away from me and does up his shirt, then grabs his jacket. Sal opens the door to his room and extends his arm. "Shall we?" he asks, offering me a smile, revealing his dimple. My body responds to him, again, and I have to fight the urge not to throw myself at him.

Walking out into the sunshine, I take a deep breath. Sal moves toward me, only to stop abruptly.

"One minute. Wait here."

He goes back inside and shuts the door. I'm stunned, but then he remerges with his jacket on and I watch as he does up the top button. Grabbing his hand, we walk hand in hand to the café. I have never felt so aroused in my life. I wish I were more experienced with men. He looks at me as though he's amused and gives me a half-smile. I'm sure Sal knows exactly what he's doing to me.

Do I respond? Do I try to make conversation? Or should I kiss him and see what happens?

All this runs through my mind as he guides me to a booth in Bettie's Café. I sit opposite him, and he continues to hold my hand.

The waitress from earlier comes bounding up to our table, and Sal says, "Hello, Rosie, how are you this morning?"

"Great! It's another glorious day in downtown Tourmaline! Now, what can I get you?" Her infectious personality bubbles over.

Sal looks at me. "Well, I think I have to try those waffles, please, Rosie."

"Fantastic choice!" she says, and winks at me. Then she looks to Sal. "The same as yesterday? And pronto on the coffee?" she says with a smile.

"Sounds good, Rosie, thank you."

As Rosie backs away, she points at Sal behind his back and gives me the thumbs up. I smile at her, and Sal turns around to see a red-faced Rosie hurrying back to the kitchen.

He raises his eyebrows at me. "I think Rosie approves." Then he runs his thumb over my knuckles, and heat pools between my thighs. I go to pull my hand from his, but he holds on. "Tell me about yourself. Where are you from? What do you do?"

For a moment, I'm caught off-guard. My senses have been so focused on him, and now he wants to know about me. I look into his eyes, and I see compassion there. I have no idea how to tell him about my life and myself, so I try turning the tables on him.

"No, you don't want to know about me, not really. I'm boring. Tell me about you and what brings you to Tourmaline."

He stares at me for a moment and is about to say something when Rosie appears with our coffees.

"Here you go!" she says, and I'm temporarily saved from any conversation.

CHAPTER 13

JONAS

I follow Emily from the compound to Doc Jordan's, then Bettie's Café, then the motel. Now she sits in Bettie's, hand in hand, with the Italian who came to the compound and asked questions about Ms. Saunders and Grinders Transport.

Is she playing with us? Do they have an agenda? What's the real reason they're in Tourmaline? All these questions flood my mind. I know one thing for sure—Dane will want to know. I wasn't lying when I said I had to go out there today, so I'd best be on my way. Dane, our president of the MC, was stabbed six weeks ago, and his woman has kept him hostage in his home, recuperating. I know he's had enough, so I organized for his woman, Kat, to go shopping today.

I stand and watch the two of them in the café for a moment longer, then head back to the compound. I'm supposed to be taking Dane for a ride to The Gorge, so he can blow out some cobwebs. Then, I was going to bring him back to the garage, and finally, to the depot to make sure he's happy with the way things are running. The club owns the garage, but Dane owns the depot. We get a cut from it, though, for doing ride-alongs to ensure the freight isn't stolen or tampered with. Dane also employs a heap of us at the depot, so it's to everyone's advantage to make sure it's running at a profit.

When I arrive back at the compound, I see Fith, and he walks toward me. He nods with determination as he keeps coming. He's a big guy who's loyal to the MC. If Dane told him to slit my throat, he'd have no problem doing it. The sick thing is, he'd do it with a smile on his face and not think twice about it. There's something in his eyes which goes from light to dark in an instant, almost as if evil waits behind them.

"Hey, VP, what gives?" he asks.

"You were here earlier when the Italian paid us a visit, weren't you?" I ask.

"Yeah, man, I was."

"I followed Emily, and she went straight to him."

He raises his eyebrows and says, "What do you want me to do?"

"Nothing for now, keep an eye on them. They're at Bettie's, and Fith, don't provoke him. I need to talk to the prez. It's his sister, after all."

He nods. "What if I order something to eat at Bettie's? It's a small town, and I eat there all the time, so it wouldn't be unusual."

"All right, but remember whose sister she is, yeah? No confrontations. You understand?" I like Fith, but you really have to spell things out.

"You got it, VP. On my way." He smiles at me, then heads toward town. I watch him go and hope he'll follow orders.

I head for my bike. The ride out to Dane's won't take long, and it's a nice ride.

Pulling into his drive, I turn off my bike, and walk toward the front door of his house, only to find him walking toward me.

I call out, "Hey, hey, Prez! Where are you off to?"

"Oh, Jonas, thank God it's you. Did you arrange for Kat to go shopping? 'Cause if you did, I owe you a fucking solid, man!"

"Had enough of Madam President, Prez?" I tease him.

"Real fucking funny! Kat won't let me do anything, and if I have to spend another day in this house cooped up without a fucking thing to do, I might fucking kill someone!"

I laugh. "I had Rebel get your bike ready. Wanna hit the Gorge?"

"Fuck, yes!" He claps me on the shoulder and practically skips across the courtyard.

"Do you want me to call her, tell her where you are?" I try to make it sound like an innocent question, but I can't help it, I laugh.

"Everyone's a fucking comedian! Let's go!"

"Wait, Prez, there's something I wanted to tell you about. A guy came into the garage yesterday, an Italian, and he started asking questions about Ms. Saunders and the depot. I followed him and saw he went back to the motel where he got a visitor."

"A visitor? Well, who the fuck was it?" Dane starts his ride, a smile spreading across his face as he listens to the sound of the engine.

"Emily."

The smile freezes in place, and he looks into my eyes, and then he kills the engine.

"What the fuck is my sister doing in town? And what the fuck is she doing with an Italian who's asking questions about Ms. Saunders?"

I shrug. "Guess we'll find out soon enough. She turned up at the compound yesterday, all busted up. Said she'd been in a car accident, and we towed her car back. It was about 170 miles out of town. Had Luke bring it back."

"Why wasn't I told?" His voice has gone steely, and his eyes blaze with anger.

"Prez, she said she wanted to surprise you. Your dad passed. She said she wanted to tell you. I took her to Doc Jordan, and he gave her something for the pain, then she passed out in my arms on Main Street. I know I should've told you earlier. That's on me."

"Fuck, Jonas. You should have told me. Where's she now? Do you have anyone following her?" he growls at me.

"When I left town, she was at Bettie's with the guy. I asked Fith to keep an eye on them."

"Okay. Let's go into town and see what gives." He looks at his bike and goes to turn it on but stops and says, "My dad passed? He's been sick a long time, and she's looked after him through all of it. Did she talk about any of it? Did she ask about me?"

"Not really, Prez. I was surprised she hadn't told you she was coming. I believed her story. She said your dad had died, and she got in her car and headed here. On the way, she swerved to miss an animal and ran into a tree. She said a stranger stopped to pick her up, and he happened to be headed here, too." He looks at me questioningly. "Dane, I know how it sounds, I know, but I believed her. She's either a really good liar, or it's happened the way she said."

"A stranger who *happens* to be headed here and just happens to want to know about our business. Not fucking likely, man. Come on, let's go into town."

I feel as if I've let him down, like I've been played.

I didn't become VP by being nice or being lied to by a pretty-fucking-face. If she's done that, she'll regret coming here—sister or not.

CHAPTER 14

FITH

Fuck. As I walk into Bettie's, I see Salvatore Agostino, Captain in the Abruzzi family. I'm fucked. The club never knew Ms. Saunders ran guns, and when she passed, it seemed like a good idea to keep it going. It was easy money for me, and the club unknowingly guards every shipment. I expanded her business as she had no interests on the East Coast—seemed stupid to me—and they were eager for product. Supply and demand, it's what Ms. Saunders used to say. It's a business like any other. I probably should've told the club, especially Dane, but the money was too good. I've now got a nice little nest egg.

I stroll up to the counter, and Rosie walks toward me. She doesn't smile at me or give me any pleasantries. It's as if she can sense what I'm really like. She came to one of the club's parties once, and I cornered her in one of the rooms. The fear came off her in waves, and I liked it. I liked how it felt to have someone so scared of me. She's not bad on the eyes—kind of a boy figure, no real ass or tits, but she has other attributes. I had her pinned in a corner, one arm on each side of her. I didn't say anything to her. I stared at her, lowered my arms, and began to undo my jeans. I smiled at her, and she looked even more scared. Then I leaned in and rubbed my face against hers, and she pushed herself further into the wall and whimpered. Then, fucking Bear walked in, and as I turned, she ran. Rosie knew what I was going to do to her, what I was going to take from her.

I lied to Jonas when I said I eat here all the time. I don't.

Now Rosie stands in front of me, and she almost shouts, "What can I get you?" The entire café turns and looks at me.

I give her my best death smile. As she shrinks away from me, I say, "Coffee and apple pie, please, *Rosie*." I drawl her name out. She nods and goes into the kitchen. She doesn't come back out, but Howie, the cook, does, and glares at me. Smiling at him, he falters in his step. Yes, he knows how dangerous I am.

"Here's your pie and coffee," he says.

"What, no ice cream?" I try to sound jovial, but he knows I'm a threat.

He grabs my pie, walks out the back, returns, and practically slams it down in front of me. I look up at him and sarcastically say, "Thank you, Howie. I've always admired those who work here." I give him a leering look, and he's visibly shaken as he takes two steps away from me.

From behind me, I hear, "Is there a problem?"

I turn, and fucking Salvatore Agostino stands behind me.

"Problem, why would you think there's a problem?" Old habits die hard, and I stand up and get in his face. Fucking Captain or not, I'm no pussy. I'm slightly taller than him, but the guy is built. We're probably the same size, but my height might give me an extra advantage.

He looks me up and down, then smirks. "I think you should leave." He opens his jacket, and I can see a glimpse of a gun. He's letting me know he's not afraid to use it. He's trying to scare me.

I laugh, really laugh. No one has gone head-to-head with me in a while. I slowly stop, then hold his gaze and let my inner demons take over as I stare at him. I'm ready. He may be a Captain in the Abruzzi family, but here in Tourmaline, we rule, and he can go fuck himself.

He cocks his head to the side, and I'm about to go on the attack when Dane's sister stands between us, putting both her hands on his chest.

"Salvatore, let's go, please. I remembered I was supposed to go see Doc Jordan. It would be rude of me not to." He looks down at her, then gives me a hard stare. "Please, Sal, can we go, please?" It sounds like a plea even to my ears. He looks at Emily, and he relinquishes.

He lets her take his hand, but as he passes me, he says, "I'll not forget this, another time?" I stare after him as he walks out onto the street, and then he's gone.

I heard he had balls of steel. I think it's time I left Tourmaline. If Dane finds out what I've been up to and the fact I haven't shared it with the club, I'm as good as dead. I pull my phone out of my jeans and dial Bear.

"Yo, Bear, it's Fith."

"Fith, what's up, man?"

"Jonas asked me to keep an eye on Emily, but I think I overstayed my welcome with her. Could you come babysit?"

Everyone knows the women of Tourmaline give me a wide berth, except for the whores, who don't have a choice. I pay them, and they earn their money with me.

"Sure, man, where is she?"

"She's headed for Doc Jordan's."

"I'm on it!"

"Thanks, man." Hanging up, I give Rosie my best

smile and stride for the door. Time to pack my things, grab my bike, and hit the road.

CHAPTER 15

DANE

It's been a long time since I've seen Emily. She was only a little kid when I was thrown out. Contact between us has been difficult because of Dad. She rang when he first got sick, and I could tell by her voice, I'd let her down when I refused to come to his bedside.

The damage that man inflicted on me haunted me for years. I made wrong choices, but I did my best not to become like him. He'd drink and beat my mother. When she fell pregnant with Emily, I'd try to protect her, but I was only seven. I tried to stand between them, but he didn't care—he would beat a seven-year-old as easily as he'd beat a pregnant woman.

I remember one night when Emily was only

little, and I must have been about ten. We all slept in a bed with Ma, and I had a knife under my pillow. We slept huddled together, waiting for him to come home, but that night he didn't. Things changed when I turned thirteen and had a growth spurt. Although I couldn't fight him, I could be more of a shield for my mother. Eventually, though, I began to hit back, and at fifteen, I knocked him to the ground. He didn't like it. He didn't like having someone who could fight for themselves, who could stand up to him. One night, he threw me out. He got into a drunken rage and started in on my mother, so I defended her with my fists, the way he taught me. I broke his nose, and he threw me out. I can still see my mother's face the night when I pleaded with her to throw *him* out, to make a stand. She grabbed Emily and walked away, leaving me in the night with the clothes on my back. Alone.

That was the last time I saw them all together. I wanted to have a relationship with Emily, and I kept tabs on her, but I wasn't getting wrapped up in my family again while he was there. In a way, it was the best thing that happened to me because I found the MC. They, unlike my real family, protected me, encouraged me, and in them, I found out what the word 'family' actually means. Now I have Kat, and with her, I'll create my own family.

I wanted to go see Emily when our mother died. She was gunned down in a robbery gone wrong.

With my connections in the MC, I tracked down those responsible for her death, and they paid with their lives. But I couldn't contact my sister, not with our father still in the picture. I wasn't letting him back into my life. Now, she's in town and I want to have a relationship with her, but will she want one with me?

I'm on my bike and headed for town. My mind full of memories of her as a child. Emily isn't a child anymore and if she's associated with this stranger, I need to know why.

Pulling into the compound, I park my bike, then stalk across the lot and head into town. Fith is parked in Main Street and looks like he's about to climb on his bike.

"Fith! Thought you were given a job to do?" I growl at him.

He looks at his bike, then at me. He slowly walks toward me. "Hey, Prez! Yeah, I was watching your sister, but got into it with that fucker, Sal. So, I asked Bear to keep an eye on her."

"Sal?" I ask

He looks at me and nods, and something flashes across his face, a look I can't decipher. "Yeah, Salvatore Agostino, he's a Captain in the Abruzzi family."

"How the fuck do you know that? Did he tell you?" I ask.

"I've seen him around when I was with the East

Coast chapter. He's a ruthless fucker, Prez."

I stare at Fith, and if I didn't know better, I'd say he was lying or nervous. He is loyal, he's proved it, but I can see he has his bike all packed up for a ride, and we don't have one planned. Could he fear this, Salvatore Agostino?

"I can see you're planning a ride, but, man, you aren't leaving town 'cause some fucker with the Abruzzi family has come to visit. So, unpack." I motion toward his bike, and he nods. "I'm going to find Emily, and when I come back, you and I are going to have a sit-down, yeah?"

"Okay, Prez. We're good, yeah?" he asks.

"We're good, man, so long as you don't leave. You're an integral part of this MC, and whatever this fucker wants, we'll sort it together."

He nods at me and walks back into the clubhouse. Something's not right.

"You okay, Dane?" Jonas stands beside me.

"He was preparing to leave. He says the stranger is Salvatore Agostino, Captain in the Abruzzi family. What would make Fith so scared he'd pack up?"

I look at Jonas, who responds, "Did he ask this Agostino who he was? I told him to watch, not interact."

I look at Jonas quizzically. "No, he said he recognized him from earlier dealings when he was with the East Coast chapter. Didn't he mention it?"

"No, Fith was in the clubhouse when the guy

came in, and I sent him to keep an eye on him and Emily. He didn't say anything about knowing him."

I look at him, then look back at the clubhouse and shake my head from side to side. Letting out a frustrated sigh, I run a hand over my face and through my hair. "Can you keep an eye on him while I go find Emily?"

"Yeah, Dane. But be careful, yeah?" He looks serious. I nod at him and head to Main Street.

I pull out my phone and dial Bear, who answers on the second ring. "Yo! Prez!"

"Hey, Bear, you got eyes on my sister?"

"Sure do, she's still with the Italian guy, and they look cozy. They're in Doc Jordan's right now."

"Cool, man. I'm on my way." I hang up, put my phone into my jacket, and walk toward my destination. Tourmaline has everything you could want. It's not a big town, but it has everything I need. I see Bear in the distance, and I'm headed toward him when I see Emily step out onto the sidewalk, hand in hand with Salvatore Agostino. He stares at her like she's the most amazing woman he's ever met, and she looks smitten too.

I close in on them, and it's as if he senses me. He turns and puts himself in front of Emily as he faces me. Then Bear walks up behind them, and I see Agostino brace, trying to decide who the biggest threat is. I nod at Bear, who stops advancing toward them. Then Agostino gives me his full attention. I see Emily trying to move around him, but he has his arm out, stopping her.

I stop when I'm about three feet away from them. "Salvatore." I nod at him. "You have someone behind you who belongs to me, to my family. I'd appreciate it if you moved, so I could greet her," I growl at him.

He looks me up and down. "She can greet you from where she is, and she doesn't belong to you."

I look past him to Emily, who looks confused. "Hello, Emily. It's been a long time, sis."

Agostino turns and looks at Emily. "You're his sister?"

She stares at him, then looks back at me and nods. Tears form in her eyes. I take a step toward her. "Em, I'm so sorry about Dad. You should've called."

"What?" she says with a high-pitched voice. "I should have called?" She takes a step toward me, bridging the gap between us. I'm six foot six, so I tower over her. "Do you know what I went through with him? Do you know how hard it was to watch him waste away, writhing around in pain? I fucking needed you to be there for me!" she screams the last few words at me and hits me with her fists. The pain is so raw in her eyes, and the tears stream down her face. She yells and hits me, and I let her. Bear goes to move, but I signal him to stay where he is. I glance at Salvatore, and he looks shocked at

Emily's outburst. Then, he places both his arms around her and takes a step back as he holds her against his body. He whispers to her in Italian, trying to soothe her.

"Em, I can see you're in pain and are mad. I understand, but you have to know I cut my ties with Dad and Mom years ago. I always wanted to have a relationship with you, Em, but he'd never allow it. You know how he was, Em. I thought you'd leave. I thought you'd come find me one day, and you have."

She stops flailing about, the tears still falling like a waterfall as Salvatore continues to hold her. She stares at me with eyes full of pain and shakes her head from side to side.

"Why did you leave me?" she whispers. "Why didn't you take me with you or come back for me? Why?" She turns away from me, burying her head into Salvatore's chest.

He looks me in the eyes and tells me, "I'll bring her to you when she has calmed down."

"No, she belongs with me."

He looks down into her eyes, seeking a response from her. She shakes her head, and I hear her whisper, "No. Sal, please."

It feels like someone winded me. My own blood doesn't want to be with me. I can't let her leave without speaking with her. "Em, I know you're mad, and you have every right to be. But, Em, you don't know the full story. You were only seven or eight when I was thrown out. I have a lot to tell you, a lot to share. Please, Em, don't leave until we've talked."

Looking up at Salvatore, she whispers to him, "Just not now. Give me a minute to get myself together."

"Give me an hour," he says, locking eyes with mine.

I concede and give her the time she needs.

A voice from behind me pulls me away from the intensity of the moment. "Is there a problem here?" It's Sheriff Morales.

I turn to look at him and say, "No, Sheriff, we're all good."

He stares past me at my sister, then he asks, "Ma'am, is he bothering you?"

She turns from Agostino's embrace to face the sheriff, finding his hand as she does. "No, I'm fine. Our father died, and I'm..." her words trail off as fresh tears form in her eyes.

"Father?" The sheriff looks from me to her and back again. "Sympathies to you both. Sorry, Dane, didn't realize you had family." I give a slight nod. He returns my gesture and continues on his way. But he stops about twelve feet away and spins back around. "Salvatore Agostino, Abruzzi crime family. What are you doing here?"

"I'm a citizen of this wonderful country and can travel it, can't I?" he growls at the sheriff.

The sheriff looks at me and says, "You get into

bed with these people and trouble comes here, I won't like it, Reynolds. That would be bad for this town."

I raise my eyebrows at the sheriff and turn so I'm facing him. "Mr. Agostino is here supporting my sister, right, Sal?"

"That's right. I've got no... business in Tourmaline."

The sheriff stands with his hands on his hips, exchanging glances between Agostino, Emily, who's still holding hands with a ruthless killer, and me.

It's clear he doesn't believe us, but at the moment, we haven't done anything wrong, so he says, "Right." He fixes Emily with a stare. "Ma'am, have a nice day." He turns and walks away from us.

I look back at Em, but she refuses to make eye contact.

I move my gaze to Agostino. "An hour, two tops. Come to the clubhouse, or I come looking for you. And trust me when I say you don't want me looking for you."

Turning on my heel, I head for the compound.

CHAPTER 16

GUIDO

I sit in my rental car with two of my best men, looking at the scene in front of me. Salvatore Agostino is holding onto Dane Reynolds' sister, and they're all chatting to the local cop. From here, it's hard to see if they're friendly with him or not. It would explain how easy it's been for them to run guns if the local law enforcement were on the take. It's not going to be easy to follow Sal around in this small town without someone recognizing me. It's why I brought the boys.

So far, I've spent a night in my car watching Sal. It's possible he's in on the gun-running and cutting us out of the deal. I have no idea what the sister has to do with anything, but from a distance, she appears to be important to both of them. A man like

Dane Reynolds wouldn't let a woman beat him up in public and not stop her if she wasn't. Perhaps she's the key.

"What should we do, Guido?" asks Vinnie, sitting next to me.

"We need to be careful. We need to keep out of sight. What's your take on the woman?" I ask.

"I'd fuck her, she's hot," says Johnnie from the back seat.

Vinnie laughs, and I agree with Johnnie. "Yeah, she is, but she could do with more meat on her." Looking back at her, I add, "But you're right, she's definitely fuckable."

"Sal seems attached to her. Never really seen him hold hands with a woman before, unless it was to take her back to his room and fuck her. You think he's been keeping this one on the side and out of sight?" asks Vinnie.

"Certainly looks like it. Call Fredo and get him to run a background check on her." Vinnie pulls out his phone and talks. I look at Johnnie in the rearview mirror. "I need a good night's sleep to find some perspective. So, you need to hang out here, keep out of sight, and watch Sal. We're going to Pearl, the next town over. I'm pretty sure the Savage Angels keep their boys here, so we should be safe to check into the motel there. We'll be back in the morning." He nods, and as he climbs out of the car, I add, "Johnnie, don't fuck this up."

He looks at me. "Yes, boss. I'll keep out of sight." He wanders off down Main Street away from Sal and disappears into the park opposite the motel.

He'd better keep out of sight. Sal can be ruthless, but I've had enough of him. He's made his way up through the ranks faster than anyone I've ever seen. He's never put a foot wrong until now. Finally, I have something on him which will upset the Don. If I can prove he can't handle the situation, or better still, he was in on it, I can make my move on him and take over his business. My boys are loyal. Even if Sal isn't in on it, we'll make it look like he was. The Don will have to agree to kill him, then. There are rules, you can't kill a Captain in the family without permission. It's a quick way to get yourself killed, no matter who you are. The Don is getting older, and my business is one of the largest in his family. He trusts me completely, and he'd never suspect I'm positioning myself to take over.

The Don has a son, Michael, but he's a moron. He has no head for business. All he's good at is fucking his whores. I'm the obvious choice for Don when the old man dies. There's no way the other Captains and heads of family will go against me when I make my move.

I'm patient.

I can wait until the old man dies. At which point, everything will be mine.

CHAPTER 17

SALVATORE

I watch Reynolds stride away from me. He's built like a mountain, all muscle and tattoos. His companion catches up with him, and together, they head for their clubhouse. I look down at Emily, nice name, but I prefer amare. I don't understand why she didn't tell me who she is. I move her toward my motel room. She's visibly upset, and the locals all stare at us as I practically drag her with me.

We stand in front of the door to my room, and I look at her as tears stain her face and her bottom lip quivers. She holds herself as she shakes. I open the door, go in and do a quick check— the bed's been made, and the room tidied. I go back out, grab her, and pull her inside, guiding her in front of the bed.

"Sit down, amare." I go into the bathroom to fill up a glass with water. When I return, she takes it from me. Her hands are unsteady as she brings it to her mouth for a small sip. Grabbing a chair near the door, I position myself in front of her. I notice she's still shaking, so I take off my jacket and place it around her shoulders, and her eyes go to my gun.

"It's for protection, nothing else. I have many enemies, and you never know when I'm going to make a new one." As I go to sit back down, she grabs my face and tries to kiss me. It's a fumbled attempt, and I end up head butting her.

"Ouch," she says as she rubs her head.

"What was that?" I say as I sit back down and rub my head.

What was left of the glass of water is now all over the floor, soaking into the carpet.

"Oh my God, I'm so sorry!" Her face is a mask of embarrassment—well, at least she's stopped crying.

I sit there as we both rub our faces and laugh. I look at her, a little concerned she's going to cry, but a smile spreads across her face, and she laughs too. I like her laugh—her entire body shakes with it.

She throws herself backward on the bed. "I'm sorry. That was a disaster. I'm so not good at this." She continues to laugh and stares at the ceiling, not realizing I've stopped.

"You're so not good at what?"

Her laughter freezes, and her eyes remain glued to the ceiling.

"Ahh... it's just I'm... awkward. I always have been."

"Awkward?" I say with a smile in my voice. I lean forward in the chair and place my hands on her knees. I feel her go completely still.

She sits up and covers both my hands with her own. "I'm sorry, I should go."

I let my hands move up her thighs, and I hear her intake of breath. I capture her eyes with mine and whisper, "How about we try it again? I'm going to kiss you. You're going to give yourself over to me, Emily, my amare. Do you understand?" She has no idea what I'm really asking her, but she'll learn. Before too long, she will understand her submission is important to me. It's who I am.

She nods at me ever so slightly, and I take the opportunity to move in on her. I slowly put my lips to hers and let my hands travel up her body to cup her face. She sighs into my mouth, and I place my hands on her shoulders and gently push her back onto the bed. I feel her small hands as they travel up my body and encircle me. I place my knee between her legs, and she opens for me. Putting some of my weight on top of her, my hand cups her breast. She's not wearing a bra, and I tweak her nipple through the dress. She arches into me, so I move my hand further down her body. All the while, our kiss intensifies, and our tongues duel.

The dress is easily pushed up, and as I explore her further, I discover she isn't wearing any panties. She moans into my mouth, and her hands tug at my shirt, trying to touch the skin beneath.

I stop and move away from her. "Awkward? No, amare, I think not. But I need to stop this before it goes any further. I have much I need to discuss with you, much I need to know. My first question is... do you always wear no panties?" I can't help the smile spreading across my face as I ask this, so I kiss the side of her cheek to mask it.

I shift to the side of her and prop my head in my hand. The blush creeping up her face is adorable. When she turns her head from mine, I reach over and turn it back, capturing her eyes with mine.

"No, it's just, I didn't pack anything. I'd been in those clothes for days, and after I had a shower, I couldn't put them back on, so I borrowed this dress and went commando."

"Commando?" I roll onto my back and laugh.

"Yes, you know, commando, no underwear..." her voice trails off. I stop my laughter and look at her.

"Amare, I know what commando means. I've never heard a woman say it before. It was funny." I chuckle.

She gives me a tentative smile and pushes the hair off her face. "I really need to go shopping."

"Hmm... yes you do, but we'll do it later. Now, tell me why you don't have any clothes with you and why you didn't tell me who you were?"

"I wasn't hiding who I was. You never even asked me my name!" I was so wrapped up in my own thoughts and trying to keep her out of trouble, I didn't ask her anything important.

Christ, am I slipping?

First, the Savage Angels move in on my gun business, then I'm continually saving this woman, and I didn't get her name, a woman who could prove useful in future negotiations. As this thought goes through my mind, I rub my face and lay on my back.

"You're right, I should've asked you your name. I don't know why I didn't." I rub my hand over my face again, trying to sort out my confused mind. "So, you're the sister of Dane Reynolds, leader of the Savage Angels." I make it a statement. All you have to do is look at them together, and you can see the family resemblance. It's strange, he's enormous, and she's tiny, but there's no doubting they're related. I turn my head to her.

"He's the whole reason I came to Tourmaline."

"You came to Tourmaline to see Dane? Why?"

It's clear Emily and Dane have a very distant relationship. I'm not even sure if she understands his position within the Savage Angels or what he stands for. I'm drawn to her. It's as though she needs protecting from the world, including her brother.

I sit up, move the chair further away from the bed, and then retake my seat. I find it easier to tell if a person is lying to me if I stare them in the eyes. "He has interfered with some of my business dealings near home. I need to work it out." She sits up and pulls her dress down over her knees. I reach over and grab her hand. "Why don't you have any clothes? Or do you keep them at your brother's?" I ask.

She pulls away from me and shakes her head. "No, I haven't seen Dane in years. He and my father had a falling out years and years ago. I've only spoken to him twice in the last ten years." She sighs and drops her gaze to her hands. "When Dad died, I wasn't thinking straight." She straightens her shoulders and locks eyes with me. "I am now, though. I need to go back home. Will you come with me when I go to see Dane? I don't know if I have the courage to see him on my own."

"Of course, I'll come with you, but you haven't told me why you have no clothes." I watch as a smile spreads across her face.

"I kind of got in my car and drove. I don't have anyone, not even friends, really. Dad made sure of that. Dane is all I have left of my family."

"Amare, I'm so sorry."

She shakes her head frantically. "Oh no, Sal, don't

be sorry for me, not that. I've had enough sympathy to last me a lifetime. It's time I started living for myself. So, starting right now, I need to buy myself some clothes, underwear included, and then I'll go see Dane with you." A frown creases her forehead.

"What is it, amare?"

"There's one small problem. I wrecked my car, so how do I leave town? Do you think they have buses?" I laugh, and so does she.

"I'll drive you to wherever you need to go. I could use the company, and you're pleasant when you aren't in trouble. After, I have business with your brother."

"Really? Are you sure? I don't want to impose."

Her eyes are wide, and I can tell she means it. It's been a really long time since a woman hasn't wanted something from me. Most of them can be paid off with a bauble or money. In my life, they serve a purpose. They're either trophies or broodmares, and they never cause me this much trouble.

"You aren't an imposition, but... you must keep out of trouble. Your brother is head of the Savage Angels, and he deserves respect. Don't hit him again. His men won't stand for it."

Emily looks thoughtful. "I've never hit anyone before. Ever. I can't believe I did it." She sounds upset with herself.

I smile at her. "Next time, aim for the jaw or his

crotch, but his chest? No, amare, it probably didn't hurt him at all."

She laughs and nods her head. "Okay, jaw or crotch. Got it!"

I laugh. "How about we go shopping before you take on the Savage Angels?" I stand and walk to my jacket.

"I don't really know a lot about them." She stands and looks at her hands. "The Savage Angels, I know who they are, but... that's about it. If you have business with Dane, do you know him?" Her eyes are almost pleading.

"No, I don't know him. He's a business associate, one I have yet to have the pleasure of dealing with firsthand. Now come, Emily, let's go shopping."

She nods at me, and I again find her hand in mine. Compared to mine, hers is small and delicate, like the rest of her. She offers me one of her disarming smiles and pulls me toward the door.

CHAPTER 18

DANE

I have my phone to my ear waiting for Judge to pick up, which he does on the fifth ring. The fucker laughs as he says, "Hey, hey, Prez, how's it goin'?"

"Judge, I need you to listen. Do you have eyes on Kat?" I growl into the phone.

"Yes, Prez, she's sitting right next to me having a latte. What's wrong?" His voice has lost all joviality, and he's now the soldier I need him to be.

"We have the Abruzzi family in town, Salvatore Agostino, to be exact. You keep my woman safe. Where are you?"

"We decided to go to Pearl County. Want us to come home?" he asks.

"Yes. I don't know why they're here or what they want, but it can't be good. I'd feel better if Kat was closer to home and me. Keep your eyes open and call if there's a problem. I'll send some of the boys to meet you. You're in her car, yes?"

Kat owns a Mustang, a muscle car. I swear my girl is going to get herself killed one of these days in a car or on a bike. She has two speeds—flat out and stop. She's like it in life too. After having that fucker try to take my woman, I keep her safe. Thank fuck, she's used to bodyguards, so she doesn't mind having a brother around. She likes Judge. They seem to have a bond. He's loyal to the MC, which means he's loyal to me, and he knows she's mine, so there isn't anything to worry about. If she has a day away from me, and I can't go with her, I usually send Judge. He has a thing with one of her band members, Jasmin, so it's not normally a problem.

"Yeah, man, we are. She wants to talk to you."

"Put her on."

"Dane, babe, what's up?" She sounds happy.

"Darlin', need you back in Tourmaline. Something has come up. I'll explain when you arrive, but I need you home, yeah?"

"Babe, you were supposed to be out with Jonas. What happened?" she asks.

"You fucking knew? Here I was thinking I'd put one over on you, and you knew?" I laugh into the phone.

"Of course, I knew! As if you could fool me, Dane Reynolds! Do I have to come home?"

"Yeah, darlin'."

"You owe me, Dane Reynolds!" She laughs into the phone. "I had an entire day planned! I'm thinking you should buy me a present to make up for it or you could use your imagination... love you, babe." She laughs as she hangs up the phone.

I put my phone into my pocket and look for Fith. I find him in the club's bar on a stool, staring straight ahead. I motion to Bear and Rebel, they walk toward me and follow me outside.

I turn around when I'm far enough away from the bar and give my instructions. "I need you two to keep an eye on Fith. He's not to leave town. Am I clear?"

They both nod, and Bear asks, "Has he done anything?"

I shake my head. "No, it's what he didn't do. He didn't tell us something, and I need to know why, so keep him in town until I do."

Rebel turns and goes back into the bar. Bear waits a heartbeat, then follows.

Jonas comes up behind me. He's been working at the garage.

"Prez."

"VP, need you to come with when I have a sit-down with Fith. Something's not fucking right there, and I don't know what it is. It feels like he's holding something back. Do you have any thoughts?" I ask.

"I agree, something's not fucking right. I don't understand why he didn't tell us about Agostino. Doesn't make sense."

I nod at him and walk toward the clubhouse. As I go through the doors, I see Fith sitting next to Bear at the bar. Bear sees me and moves to position himself near the door. Bear is my Road Captain. He organizes all the runs. He's efficient, and he is huge in size. He also loves to gossip, but he can keep his tongue if asked to.

I sit on a stool next to Fith.

"Wanna tell me the fucking truth about Agostino? Tell me why you didn't tell Jonas about him?" My voice is steady and full of authority. I'm the president of the Savage Angels, and I didn't get here by being a fucking pushover.

He stares at me before glancing at Jonas, who stands beside me. "I wasn't sure it was him until I went into the café. He's ruthless. He is a Captain in the Abruzzi family."

"You've already told me that." I pause and look at him in the mirror behind the bar. "Tell me why he's got you so spooked? Tell me why you're all packed up to fucking leave." I growl at him.

"Prez, I've been a loyal member for years," he says, staring back at me in the mirror. "If I've made a mistake, I'd hope you and Jonas would take it into consideration."

Now I'm fucking confused. I have no idea what

the hell he's talking about. "Are you asking for leniency before you tell me what you've done..." My pulse picks up, and I try harder to remain calm and in control. "Answer this... would you forgive the sin? Would you spare you if the tables were turned?"

"Prez, we need to call Church," Jonas interrupts before Fith has a chance to answer.

I nod and look at Fith. "Whatever the fuck you've done, you better not have betrayed the MC. If you've endangered us..." I shake my head at him and stand. In a voice everyone in the clubhouse can hear, I say, "Call everyone, Church in two hours. Fith isn't to leave the clubhouse."

I stalk outside into the sunshine, rolling my head, trying to ease the tension in my neck. The fresh air does little to help. It's my first day back, and it feels like everything has gone hay-fucking-wire. Fith is the last person in the MC who I thought would betray us. He's a good soldier, and I thought he was loyal to me.

If I'm wrong about him, can I trust anyone?

CHAPTER 19

JUDGE

Kat climbs into the car and buckles her seat belt. I look around and take note of a rental car. It's odd for tourists this time of year. In the winter, the place is flooded as is Tourmaline—the skiing is fantastic. There are two men in the car, and they're wearing suits.

"Judge? Are we going?" asks Kat.

"Mind if we take a detour, sugar?" I drawl.

"No, but Dane won't like it," she says matter-of-factly.

"I only want to see where the car went and who's in it. Is that cool?"

"Judge, if you think they're a problem, I'm all for it. I don't want my man stabbed again." She holds my gaze and continues, "Or hurt or anything? Do

Savage Fire

you understand?"

I smile at her. "Sugar, it could be some tourists. I want to get their photo to show Dane, okay?"

She nods, and I put the car in gear and follow the suits to the motel in Pearl. We watch as two men climb out of the car. I get my phone out and take a few pictures of them. They're armed—you can tell by the way their jackets sit. The older guy is obviously in charge, conveyed by the way he walks. They both do a sweep with their eyes but miss us. At least, I think they do.

"Did you get what you needed?" asks Kat.

"Yeah, sugar. Let's get this show on the road. Prez won't like me much if I don't get you home." I grin at her and hand over my phone as we head for Tourmaline. "Could you forward all the photos I took to Dane? Don't want to have an accident with you in the car."

They might be tourists, but tourists don't normally carry.

My phone rings and I look at Kat. "Who is it?"

"It's Luke. Want me to answer it?" she asks. I nod at her. "Hey, Luke, it's Kat."

"Ahh, hey, Kat, is Judge there?" he asks.

"He is, but he's driving. Can I give him a message?"

"Tell him Dane has called Church."

"Okay, Luke, will do. See you soon." She hangs up and looks at me. "He said to tell you Dane has called Church."

"Well, sugar, it's going to be one of those days."

CHAPTER 20

GUIDO

I notice the Mustang idling on the street, but it doesn't stay there for very long. Vinnie goes in and talks to the old guy in the motel. He rents two rooms, as I don't like to share. As we walk toward the rooms, my phone rings—it's Johnnie.

"Hey, boss, Sal bought that chick a whole wardrobe, even got her shoes. No way is she just a fuck. Has Fredo gotten back with intel yet?"

"No, Fredo hasn't gotten back. What's his behavior with her? Is he still holding hands?" I look up at Vinnie and indicate for him to stop. I need him to hear what's going on.

"He's either holding her hand or touching her. He's treating her like a wife, like someone he cares about. Never seen Sal do this with anyone," says Johnnie.

"Well, well, well... fucking Salvatore Agostino has a woman. You been keeping out of sight?" I ask.

"Yes, boss, no one has seen me. I know how to stay invisible."

"If there's an opportunity, take the woman." Vinnie's eyes widen, and I continue, "She'll be a valuable bargaining tool."

"Separating her from Sal isn't going to be easy, boss." Johnnie points out.

"Wait for her to be alone, then seize the moment. Don't be seen, Johnnie. Understand?"

"Yeah, boss, I understand, but what if she's not alone?"

"Only take her if she's alone." I grin at Vinnie. "As an incentive for you, you can have her first."

"I'll see what I can do, and thanks, boss." Johnnie chuckles into the phone before he hangs up.

"Is it a smart move to fuck with Sal's woman? He won't like it," Vinnie offers.

"He'll be dead. I've had enough of this fucker moving up the ranks so quickly. Why not play with his woman for a bit? It'll be fun." I open my room and go in. I'm hard, thinking about playing with her. I wonder if this town has any whores I could play with. It's probably best to lie low, but I'm horny now.

CHAPTER 21

EMILY

I'm in the small dress boutique, and Salvatore has made me try on almost every dress they have. There's no way I can afford to buy all of them. I walk out of the change room in the dress I borrowed from the Savage Angels as Salvatore pays the very excited owner for all of them.

"Sal! I can't let you pay for all of this! I wasn't going to buy them all!" I practically scream at him.

"It's done, amare. Now, do you need anything else?" His voice is calm, and he acts as if he's purchased me a coffee, not hundreds of dollars' worth of clothes.

"Yes, I need shoes, but I'm paying for them! You have to let me pay you back!" I feel my face burn with embarrassment.

"No." He flicks his eyes to the boutique owner. "Where's the nearest shoe shop?"

"It's three stores down, that way." She points and gushes. "Thank you so much. I don't normally have this kind of business unless it's tourist season!"

Sal smiles at her. Her smile becomes bigger, and she blushes. He seems to have this kind of effect on women, me included. I clear my voice, and both of them stare at me.

"No? What does no mean?" I have one hand on my hip, and I point at him with the other.

He laughs, and it rumbles up and out of his very well-defined chest. "Amare, it means no. It means I'm paying, and you're going to let me, no."

"I'm going to let you?" I can't believe he laughed at me.

"Yes, it would be my honor to buy you anything and everything you would like, especially after the terrible loss you have recently suffered." He walks to me, puts both of his hands on my face, then leans in and kisses my nose. The boutique owner sighs, and I feel like doing it as well, but I can't let him buy me all of these clothes without paying him back.

"Sal—"

"No, just no. Shall we go?" He turns to the owner and asks, "Can you have these delivered to room five at The Country Inn, please?"

She nods so enthusiastically, I think her head is about to come off. "I'll do this personally! Not a thing to worry about!" Her smile is so huge, and she looks at me and says, "This one's a keeper, honey. Don't let him go!"

I smile at her as Sal grabs my hand, and we head toward the shoe shop.

"So, what do you think, amare? Am I a keeper?" he asks, a smile playing at his lips.

"No," I say with as much force as I can muster.

"No?" He stops us both and turns me to face him. His face is serious as he asks, "Why no?"

"Because I don't need you to buy me things. I don't need to be bought. I can buy my own damn clothes and shoes! Just not as many!"

A look crosses his face, and then he laughs. "Not as many?" he says and grabs me around my waist and puts his forehead to mine.

"Sal! This is serious!" I yell at him as I batter his chest with my hands.

He stops laughing. "Yes, it is. I'm not buying you, amare. I can see you can't be bought with things. I can't promise you I will stop buying you things as it pleases me. But I see your point, okay?" His voice is deep and full of emotion. My head betrays me, and I nod. He smiles, grabs my hand again, and we continue to the shoe shop.

As we enter, the girl behind the counter is on the phone, and I hear her say, "They've arrived, gotta go." It's obvious the boutique owner has phoned her.

"Hello! I'm Bianca. Marie just phoned to tell me what color shoes would best suit the clothes you bought." I smile at her but am dying inside. Clearly, this is a big deal to this small town.

"That was nice of her. I'm a size seven. Shall we see what you have?"

Smiling, she directs me toward a chair. "Take a seat, and I'll find you some shoes to try on." She turns to grab a selection of shoes off the wall.

I look at Sal, who's trying not to laugh, and I can't help it, I smile at him. His laughter stops, and he grabs my face and kisses me. I feel my body melt into his. My hands betray me and encircle his waist as I pull him into me. Laughter bubbles up out of the shop assistant, and I remember we're in public. Sal pushes away from me with a smirk on his face, and a sigh escapes me. The heat of his body leaves mine, and I miss it. His phone rings, so he drops his hands from my face and steps further away from me to answer.

"I must take this. Will you excuse me?" I nod at him as he walks outside to take his call.

"Marie was right, he's all kinds of sweet goodness!" says Bianca, who stares at him longingly.

"Sweet goodness?" I giggle. "Yeah, he is."

We both stare at him as he turns and catches us ogling him. He does a two-finger wave and steps out onto the sidewalk.

"Shoes, Bianca, I need shoes. I only have the pair I'm wearing, so what have you got?"

"Yes, ma'am! I bet I have a few you're going to love!"

CHAPTER 22

SALVATORE

I'm on the phone with Tony. "No, I haven't had a sit-down with the Savage Angels yet. There's been a development."

"What kind of development?" he asks.

"I'm not sure yet. A woman."

His voice is full of laughter as he says, "A woman? Geez, boss. You went all that way to find a woman? Hell, you know my sister is single now, the douchebag has finally left."

I smile into the phone. "Your sister is crazy, Tony. No, this one is different. But she's the sister of the head of the Savage Angels."

"And you think my sister is crazy?"

"Your sister is crazy. I'm seeing the Savage Angels in about an hour. I'll ring you after. Okay?"

"Yeah, and, Sal, be careful. I don't understand why the family wants you to do this alone. Doesn't make sense. Watch your back."

"Agreed, doesn't make sense. Maybe it's a test from the old man. I've heard rumors he wants to expand. Maybe he's seeing if I can handle myself," I reply.

"Everyone fucking knows you can handle yourself, boss. You have been proving that since you were fifteen-fucking-years-old," he says and hangs up.

He's right. It doesn't make sense for me to be out alone. I'm a Captain in this family, I've killed, I've beaten, and I've taken. I have already proven myself. I should call the old man. I turn and see Emily with the sales assistant, laughing as she tries on shoes. She's different. I like this woman. I haven't liked a woman this much in a long, long time. She sees me looking through the window and motions for me to come inside. Pushing open the door, I hear her laughter, and it goes through me stirring up long-forgotten feelings.

"Sal! Bianca is unbelievable! She thinks I need all of these shoes! I don't have room in my closet for all of these!"

"Bianca?" She looks at me and nods. "Pack them all up, she'll have them all." Both women stop their laughter and stare at me.

"Oh, I was having some fun, sir. She doesn't have

to buy them all. I was only playing around!" says Bianca, as her mouth hangs open.

"No, Sal! I couldn't possibly buy ten pairs of shoes!" says Emily.

"Actually, there are twelve," corrects Bianca.

"Pack them up, Bianca, and have them delivered to room five at The Country Inn." I hold Emily's gaze as she shakes her head, and I smile at her. I understand why she wouldn't want me to buy her things. Since she doesn't want anything from me and has no idea who I am, what's the harm? I have more money than I can spend, and the few hundred dollars on clothes and shoes will not break my bank account. I've been careful with my money. I have planned, and I have invested. I own property all over. I don't need to work if I don't want to, but I enjoy being in charge. I like having power over my enemies. I like control in everything, including my women.

"No! I can't afford so many pairs of shoes and dresses! Sal, it will take me forever to pay you back." She has her hands on her hips, and her eyes are ablaze.

"Emily, please, it's my pleasure to do this for you. Now come, we have much to discuss before our meeting." At the sound of her name, she relaxes. Her eyes still burn, but she slowly nods her head.

"Wow, do you have a brother?" asks Bianca.

I laugh at her. "Yes, but he's doing a stint for

murder. He isn't as smart as me." Both women look shocked and are unsure if I'm serious. I walk to the cash register and look at Bianca. "Time to pay, yes?"

Bianca rushes to the counter and gives me a tentative smile. "Is it cash or credit?"

We're seated in Bettie's Café, and as usual, I'm facing the front door. Emily has been quiet since we left the shoe store. We have given our orders to Rosie, and the silence is becoming deafening.

When she blurts out, "Your brother killed someone?" Her voice is slightly raised, and she looks alarmed.

"Ahh, my brother, this is why you're quiet? Yes, he killed a man who would've eventually killed him. It's a long story, and I don't want to talk about it at the moment. I need to know about you, Emily. I need to know why you're here and what you intend to do."

"Sal, I've told you why I'm here. I came to see... no, to hurt Dane. I wasn't thinking clearly. My father was a... difficult man. When he died, I thought of Dane. He's my only living relative, but I haven't seen him since I was a kid. I have no idea what I was thinking." She sighs and fiddles with her dress.

"Your mother, where is she?" I ask.

"My mother was gunned down in a stupid robbery. The kid didn't even think the gun was loaded. She was telling him to think about what he was doing, and he panicked, pointed the gun at her, and pulled the trigger." Tears well up in her eyes. "People talk about the right to bear arms, but when they lose someone to a senseless murder, let's see how much they believe in it. If gun control were tougher, my mother would still be alive."

I lower my head, reach across the table, and grab her hand. "I'm sorry, amare. How long ago?" I feel a deep sense of loss for her. If she knew running guns was part of my business, would she still be interested in me?

"It was five years ago. My father was always a drunk, but Ma kept him in line most of the time." She looks down at the table, and a single tear escapes her eye and runs down her face. Before I can say anything, she continues, "You see, I didn't have anyone. He was all I knew. I tried to leave and went to college, but there was no one to look after him. What was I supposed to do?" Her eyes look at me pleadingly. "He was a hard man. The cancer took him. I've wondered if it was because he was so mean or if it was the bad coming out of him or turning back on him. Does it make any sense?"

I understand. There was a time I thought I had to

stay, but I took control of my own destiny and carved a path for myself. She needs to do the same. She needs to find her own way. I pass her a napkin to wipe her tears away.

"I understand, Emily, I do. My father was a difficult man as well, and unlike your mother, mine was... weak."

"Why are you here, Salvatore?" she asks.

Suddenly, I feel ashamed of my business. It is one of many, but it's profitable and brings the family much wealth. "Your brother is infringing on one of my businesses. I was sent to sort it out. I'm a Captain in the Abruzzi family, do you know of them?"

"Abruzzi family? No, I've never heard of them. What's a Captain?"

I sigh and run both hands through my hair. I'm about to respond when Rosie appears with food. She places it in front of us and asks, "Do you two want pie later? You look like you could use pie. We have a really good apple pie." Before either of us can respond, she continues, "I'm going to get you both some with ice cream." She winks at me and walks away.

"Emily—"

"I think I like it better when you call me amare," she says with a smile.

"Amare, a Captain means I'm high up in the Abruzzi family. We're organized. We run most of the East Coast."

"What does that mean, you run most of the East Coast? It sounds like a gang." She nervously laughs.

"Not a gang, a family." I pause and grab both her hands. "Organized crime, amare. We have a hand in a lot of pies. Not drugs, we're forbidden to become involved in narcotics, but we have a hand in everything else."

"Guns?" she asks.

"It's the reason I'm here. Your brother is interfering in my business, and we need to know why." Shock quickly spreads across her features.

"Guns?" she repeats her question.

"Yes." At this moment, I wish I were a different man. The choices I've made helped to carve me into the person I am today, but this person may not be someone she'll want to be with.

"Do you have to sell guns? Could you not do something else?" she asks.

"I do many other things, it's one of many." Her face scrunches up, and she appears to be lost in her own thoughts. "I feel a connection with you, one I have not had with anyone else in a long time. Take some time to think about what you know, think about how you feel about me and what I do. For now, let's eat."

Emily slowly stands. "No, I need to clear my head. Please, don't follow me. I need time to process this. You aren't who I thought you were." She sighs, her disappointment in me obvious. "I have to go see Dane to sort out our relationship." Emily turns and walks out of the café.

It shouldn't matter to me what this woman thinks. I've only just met her. I have rescued her twice and intervened in her family affairs. She wouldn't fit into my world. As I eat my meal, I can't help but wish perhaps she could fit or, at the very least, I could fit into her life.

Now she knows the truth about me, and a part of me knows she'd be better off without me.

CHAPTER 23

DANE

It's time for Church, and all the brothers who are in or around Tourmaline are here. It's unusual, but three nomads have arrived in town—Kade, JJ, and Zeke. They're practically a small MC in themselves. One can rarely be found without the other two.

"Prez, we heard Church had been called, so here we are," Kade speaks for all of them. He'd make a good president of another chapter.

"Kade, brother, it's been a while." I smile and grab his hand.

"Sounds like you've got trouble, Prez," says Kade, while JJ and Zeke nod in agreement.

"It's Fith. He hasn't divulged what he's done, but he's asked for leniency, which means he's fucked over the club in some way." Kade's eyes widen, and

I say, "Judge sent through these photos he took of two guys in Pearl. You recognize them?"

Kade shakes his head and hands my phone to JJ, who shakes his head in the negative, but Zeke looks at Kade, eyebrows raised. "What?" I growl out.

His eyes move to me. "That's Guido Lamberti. He's the enforcer for the Abruzzi family. He's a fucking killer, Prez."

"Fuck." I sigh, running my hand through my hair. "Do you know who the other one is?" He shakes his head no. "Let's go sit down and hear what Fith has to say. Today, you three are allowed to vote." It's not normal to let nomads have a say in club business, but I might need the votes, and they've always been loyal to Tourmaline and me.

As we're about to enter the clubhouse, Kat's Mustang pulls in with three bikes following. I motion for the nomads to go ahead, and I go meet Kat.

As she climbs out of the car, I grab her. "Darlin', sorry to cut your shopping short. I'll make it up to you."

"It's okay, babe, I can shop any day. So, can you tell me what's up?"

I shake my head and say, "Maybe later. I need you to go hang in the garage for a bit. I'd appreciate it if you stayed in the compound, okay?"

"Okay, I can do that. There's probably a mountain of paperwork to file." Kat smiles, but I can tell she isn't happy.

"Darlin', what if, when we're finished, I ask some of the boys to drop you at your home? That way you can supervise all the rework you have going on there." Kat's smile brightens, and she nods her head excitedly.

"That would be better! Thank you, babe." She wraps her arms around my neck and kisses me. I push her up against the car and deepen the kiss, then I hear wolf-whistles. I stop, look at her, and grin. Kat's not a piece of ass to show off. She is mine, only mine.

"Go to the garage. Stay there, yes?" It sounds like an order, and in true Kat fashion, she lets me know she's not impressed.

"Okay, babe, going to the garage." She salutes me and walks across the lot. Judge stands there, openly watching her ass and grinning.

I clear my throat, and he looks at me. "Prez, she has a nice walk." His cheeky-assed grin grows bigger. I know he's trying to get a rise out of me, and it's working.

"How about you keep your eyes off her ass, or I'll have them removed," I growl at him.

He laughs and walks toward me. "Aw, Prez, you have to know I like Kat, but I don't like Kat. She does have a great ass, though." I glare at him, and he holds up his hands. "I understand your point, and I'll rein it in."

I nod, and we both head for the clubhouse doors.

Sitting at the head of the table, I have Jonas to my left, Dirt, my Sergeant-at-Arms, to my right, and next to him is Bear. On the other side, next to Jonas, is Keg, he's our Secretary/Treasurer. Fith sits at the other end of our table. All the patched-in members, nomads, and prospects are gathered around the room. Those who can't sit at the table, stand on either side of it behind a brother.

"You're all here to listen to the wrongs Fith has brought down on the club. I don't know all of his deceit, only he withheld information regarding a Captain in the Abruzzi crime family. I have also discovered Guido Lamberti is in town."

All eyes go to Fith as he stands and looks around the room. "I've been in this club since I was nineteen. I'm the guy you go to whenever you want something done and can't or won't do it." His gaze settles on me. "I'm the keeper of many secrets. I know where all the bodies are buried. I know who we've fucked with and who we continue to fuck with."

Dirt stands and says, "Are you fucking threatening us, you motherfucker?" He slams his fist down on the table, spittle spraying from his mouth. His eyes are bulging, and the scar which runs from his temple looks like it's pulsing.

"No, brother, I'm not. I am explaining I have been loyal. I'm trying to say I made a mistake. Once it started, I didn't know how to stop it, and I couldn't go back." Fith's voice is almost a whisper as he stares at Dirt, and if I didn't know better, I'd say he was hurt. Not likely, I've seen him go from killer to best friend too many times to count.

"What have you done?" Dirt asks as he takes his seat again.

The whole clubhouse is quiet. "It wasn't me who started it. It was Ms. Saunders." A rumble goes around the room. Ms. Saunders was Kat's Ma. She owned the depot—Grinders Transport. When she died, she left the depot to me. The club acts as security for the trucks to make sure they have safe passage, and I pay them for it, but the rest of the money earned by the depot belongs to me.

"Explain yourself, Fith. What did Ms. Saunders start?" I ask in an authoritative tone.

"Do you remember when the sheriff did raids on the clubhouse and the transport company?" I nod. "The day before the raid, Ms. Saunders came and did a clean of the clubhouse with a couple of workers from the depot. She found guns, smack, and a DVD in my room." His nervousness is apparent as he looks at Jonas. "I recorded the interrogation of that guy, and I enjoyed watching it." Jonas stands up so quickly his chair flies into the brother who stands behind him, and he strides toward Fith. He grabs him by his wife-beater and walks him backward, straight into a wall.

"You stupid fucking bastard! Where is it? Where the fuck is it?" Jonas is more than angry. I've never seen him lose his control like this. Fith has his hands up and isn't fighting back as Jonas continues to slam him against the wall.

As Dirt stands up and moves to intervene, he shouts, "Jonas, brother, calm down!"

I give Kade a nod, so he, JJ, and Zeke move in to help. As Jonas is pried away from Fith, Fith says, "When she died, I found it and destroyed it. It no longer exists! She promised no copies were made, and I've never been able to find any, so I have to believe it. I have to!"

"Does someone want to tell me what you two are talking about?" I ask in a level tone, and the clubhouse goes quiet. Jonas moves back to his chair—still highly agitated—and stares straight ahead, avoiding all eye contact with me. I continue to stare at him until he slowly moves his head in my direction, but he still avoids my eyes.

"When Ray was killed by the Road Hellions, I wanted revenge. Someone had to have tipped them off he was going to be on his own. I asked Fith to find that person. He did, and together we... interrogated him." His eyes flick to mine, and all I can see is a darkness in him I've never seen before. It explains why he was away so long—he had demons to battle.

I nod and look at Fith. "Okay, so Ms. Saunders

found guns, smack, and a DVD, so what?" Dirt forcibly helps him back to his seat before returning to his.

"You all think Ms. Saunders was this sweet, little old lady, but she wasn't. You have no idea what she was capable of."

He stares at me, and I shake my head. "Fith, I knew Ms. Saunders. What the fuck are you on about?"

"She used the DVD against me. She blackmailed me into helping her, and she made me keep it from you. From the club. Ms. Saunders knew Jonas didn't know he was being filmed, so I couldn't tell you!" He's visibly upset, but I can't believe it. "Dane, she was running guns and using us to keep the shipments safe. With every Carnival Cigarette shipment, she had a shipment of guns. It was flawless. No one messed with the shipments as we were protecting them, and when she died, I expanded her business. It was easy money. There's always a demand for illegal guns. I used the contacts she already had and kept it going. It's easy money, Prez."

"How much?" I growl.

His eyes bulge out of his head as he replies, "Twenty-five thousand a week in the beginning, but I expanded to the East Coast. She had no dealings there, so I've nearly doubled the take. I'm up to forty-eight."

The room is silent. We don't run anything out of Tourmaline. It's home and off-limits. You don't shit where you eat. We all know this. I can't comprehend Ms. Saunders running guns, but I know Fith isn't smart enough to do it alone. At least now I know why Salvatore Agostino and Guido Lamberti are here.

I look around the room, and everyone stares at me. "We. Do. Not. Run. Anything. Out. Of. Tourmaline." I pause between my words, making my point clear. "We all know this. I need time to process this and have a sit-down with Salvatore Agostino. Dirt, Jonas, I expect you to sit in on it, and if everyone agrees, so we have some perspective... Kade, JJ, and Zeke." A rumble goes around the room, and I look at Bear.

He clears his throat. "Agreed!" I smile at him. He knows when to be a good soldier. "Anyone opposed?" he asks and looks around the room. "Good! Prez, how long do you think you'll need?"

"Give us two hours, and then I want you all back here." They all file out, taking Fith to a backroom. I'm left with Jonas, Keg, Dirt, and Rebel.

Keg has always been good with numbers, it's why he's the Treasurer as well as Secretary. "Ms. Saunders has been gone for what, a year and a half? If Fith is telling the truth, how much has he made?"

He looks at me, thinks a moment, and says, "One point nine-five, minimum."

"Where the fuck does he have it stashed? It's a lot of green to have lying around," I say.

"We could simply ask him." All eyes go to Rebel. "What? The fucker has to know where it is."

"Rebel is right, we should ask him," says Jonas.

"We will, but first, you want to share about the... interrogation?"

Suddenly Jonas is agitated. He paces, his gaze is riveted to the floor. I never sanctioned an interrogation. I did sanction retaliation against the Road Hellions. We wiped out thirty of them, and they called a truce. They really had no choice—we had greater numbers. I never understood why they took out Ray and only Ray. I look at Jonas, and I wonder if he knows. He took Ray's death harder than the rest of us. He's my best friend, and I know him, but his reaction to Ray's death and the way he blamed himself has never sat right with me.

"Someone had to pay for Ray's death," Jonas says as he continues to pace, not looking at any of us.

"They did pay, brother, we took out thirty of them. Don't you remember?"

He stops and looks at me. "It was my fault. It should've been me. I was supposed to be there." He shakes his head. "I had to find out who was behind it. It was a stupid mistake. You asked me to check on the fucking strip club in Marlow. I didn't want to do it because I was seeing Addy that night." I raise my eyebrows at him. I had no idea he'd been seeing

Adelynn. "She didn't want anyone to know, and more importantly, Addy didn't want Ben to know unless it was going to be serious. She didn't want him to become attached and for me to walk away, which I fucking did after Ray."

"Brother, are you saying the Road Hellions wanted to take you out, not Ray?" says Dirt.

"Yes, I disrespected their VP on their home turf. I was fucking with him, Prez. I didn't know who he was, and I gave him a beat-down in front of some of their prospects. He wasn't wearing his cut. The prospects didn't even try to step in. He was a mouthy motherfucker, and he spat on my cut, so I fucking taught him a lesson. I didn't know. I found out after Ray."

"The order for you to check out Marlow came from me. Who the fuck betrayed us?" I ask.

"There was a hang-around, his name was Flick. I used to give him shit about his name. I guess he had enough of me. He was never going to become a prospect, he was a fucking tool. He saw an opportunity to get rid of me, and he thought he'd finally become a prospect. He told the Road Hellions where I'd be and I'd be alone." He puts his hands on his hips and looks at me. "So, you see, Prez, it was my entire fucking fault. They killed Ray because they thought it was me. With Fith's help, I captured a member of their MC and tortured him until he gave up Flick, then I put him and Flick in the fucking ground." His voice cracks at the end, his eyes are red, bring his demons to the forefront.

"Brother, I can see how you'd blame yourself. If you got into a fight with any motherfucker, and our prospects were near, what the fuck do you think they'd do? There's no fucking way they'd let you get beat down by a rival MC. The guy, whoever the fuck he was, didn't have the respect of his men. You, my brother, do. It's time to let it go." He nods, turns around, and tries to get himself under control. The room is quiet.

I glance at Dirt, who looks at the ground. He sighs, pulls a chair out, and sits down. "Everyone, take a fucking seat. That explains the DVD. Now, do we all really believe Ms. Saunders is capable of what Fith is saying? I, for one, do not." He slams both hands down on the table and looks around the room.

"She knew people. I always thought it was strange. She knew the leader of the crew in Marlow. I took her shopping over there once, and I couldn't understand why he was showing her such respect. At the time, she told me he was an old family friend. She told me to leave her, and she'd ring me when she was done. Didn't make any fucking sense, but it was Ms. Saunders, so I did as she asked. I watched them for a while. They talked for a long time. I should've said something," says Rebel, as he too pulls out a chair and sits down.

"Anyone else have a story to tell?" I ask.

My men all take seats, Jonas back to my left and Dirt to my right. As they take their seats, Kade wanders in.

"Prez, Agostino is on the lot. Want me to bring him in or make the fucker wait?"

I look at the men seated at the table. "Should we bring him in? Try to sort this fucking mess out?" They all nod, and I say to Kade, "Bring him in, brother, and take a seat with us. Bring your boys, too. We could use a different perspective on this."

He nods and leaves to get Agostino.

We're all seated around the table, and I've put Agostino at the other end, facing me. He's a powerhouse. You can tell by the way he moves, he can handle himself. Dirt pats him down and finds two guns, and then he willingly gives up a third Dirt missed—it's to show he can be trusted. He doesn't have my sister with him. I have much to talk to her about and it angers me he's kept her from me. He holds my gaze as he arranges himself in the chair.

"So, Reynolds, how did the family reunion go?"

"What the fuck are you talking about?" I growl at him.

"Emily, your sister, is what I'm talking about." He leans forward.

"I thought you were bringing her with you."

"She left me over an hour ago and said she was coming here. Are you saying you haven't seen her?" His voice rises as he speaks.

"Emily hasn't set foot in this compound. If she had, I'd know about it," I say to him and look at Jonas. "Go find her. Bring her to me no matter what, understood?"

Jonas nods, stands, and looks at Agostino. "Where did you last see her?"

"We were in Bettie's Café. She said she was coming to see Dane. The only other person in town she knows is Adelynn at the motel. Perhaps she went there?"

Jonas nods and taps Rebel on the shoulder as he stands, and they both go in search of Emily. I look at Agostino, he looks perplexed, and I raise my eyebrows at him.

"We had a disagreement. I know she wasn't looking forward to seeing you, but why wouldn't she come here and face you?" Concern laces his tone.

"You had a disagreement? What about?" I ask.

"About my businesses, she was… surprised at some of my endeavors."

I frown and look around at my men. "What brings a Captain of the Abruzzi family all the way out here by himself?"

"I didn't know you were involved in running guns. I had an agreement with Christina Saunders. She assured me she wouldn't expand her interests to the East Coast. I should've known it was the Savage Angels who were in charge all along. After her sit-down with Don Dominic, she would have told you of our bargain. I'm here to find out why you would break this deal and potentially declare war with the Abruzzi family."

I'm shocked, but I keep my face a mask of neutrality. I look at Dirt, and thankfully, he has done the same.

The last thing we need is a war with the Abruzzi family. They do deals with many other rival MC's, not to mention the gangs in rougher neighborhoods across the states. He stares at me, and I know I need to answer him, but I have no fucking idea what to say. Ms. Saunders ran guns, and we stupidly guarded every shipment. I never once suspected her of anything. She looked like a grandmother, and she cooked us muffins, for fuck's sake. How the hell did she get involved in guns and God knows what else? I need to regroup, I need to talk to Kat to see what she knows, and I need some fucking intel on Ms. Saunders.

"Before we start, we need a drink. What will you have?" I do my best to stall.

"Coffee, black, no sugar," he says as he slouches back into his chair.

Standing up, I move further into the clubhouse, and Dirt follows. I run my hand through my hair for the umpteenth time today.

"Need you to do a background check on Ms. Saunders. Find me something, fucking anything, and do it quickly."

"You believe him?" asks Dirt.

"I don't know what the fuck I believe. We have a brother doing deals for over a year, and none of us knew. How does it happen? Do the background check, and I'll go talk to Kat, she has to know something." I glance at Kade, who stands up and makes his way toward me.

"Kade, I need you to entertain him, make his coffee, and keep him busy while I go talk to Kat."

"Prez, you need to talk to your woman?" He places his hands on his hips, clearly wondering what the fuck I'd need to discuss with my woman. Thankfully, he has the sense not to question me any further.

Moving into his space, my face a mere inch from his, I growl, "It's a long story, Kade. *Trust me.*"

Kade drops his hands and moves back. His eyes widen slightly and he dips his head.

It might be my first day back, but no one

questions me in my clubhouse. Even those I respect.

As I walk into the office of the garage, Kat is sitting on the desk watching television.

She yells out, "Finally! A girl could starve!" She turns and laughs when she sees me. "Sorry, babe, thought you were Howie. I asked him to bring me the house special." She leaps off the table and into my arms, and in her best seductive voice, which threatens to bring me to my knees, says, "Do you have anything I could... eat, babe?" Damn, the way she licks those lips. I know she's kidding, but my dick doesn't—it's rock-hard. I move us into the office and sit her on the table before quickly locking the door and pulling the blinds.

"Dane! What are you doing? Come on, babe, Howie is—"

"Darlin', you shouldn't tease me unless you're willing to keep up your end of the bargain."

I spread her legs and position myself between them. Cupping her face, I kiss her deeply. She responds to me as she always does. Kat wraps her legs around me, and as I move one of my hands to her breast and rub my thumb over her nipple, she moans into my mouth. I trail kisses from her mouth and slowly travel to the hollow of her neck. Dropping to my knees, I'm in front of her jean-clad core. My hand travels the inside of her thigh until I reach her center, and she responds to my thumb as I caress her.

"Darlin', from now on, unless you're on the back of a bike, could you please wear dresses or skirts?"

She giggles. "Honey, if you're willing, I could have these off in the blink of an eye!"

"No, you have Howie coming, and I need to ask you some questions about your ma."

She grabs me by the ears and pulls me up. "What do you want to know about her? And, baby, you owe me after that!" She laughs again and kisses me.

I wrap my arms around her. "Dresses or skirts or no fun for you," I tease.

She laughs and slaps my chest. "You don't tell me what to wear! And I was nice to you in front of the boys, but I don't like being told to stay here!" She smiles, but she's letting me know she doesn't appreciate my overprotectiveness.

"Darlin', I'll always try to keep you safe, and believe me, keeping you here and knowing you're safe is more for me than you."

I place my forehead to hers, and she kisses me. "I know you mean well, but I'm a capable woman. Just 'cause I got kidnapped once doesn't mean it will happen again." Then she bursts into laughter, and I do the same.

"Thank you for following my lead outside when you got home. Darlin', how much did you know about your ma's business interests?"

"Nothing. I didn't even know she'd bought Grinders Transport, remember?" She has a puzzled look on her face.

I place my hands on her shoulders and ask, "Do you know of anyone who would?"

"Dave. He handled almost everything in my life, so he'd know about Ma. He runs background checks on everyone, probably did one on you, too." She winks and smiles at me.

"Dave, I should've fucking known." Dave is Kat's manager. We're still getting to know each other, but I keep his princess happy, so for now, he likes me. "Darlin', do you have his number? I have a few questions for him about Grinders."

"Yep, I do, baby. It's in my phone, which is in my handbag, which is in the other room. But..." She draws this out.

"But what?" I ask.

"But you owe me," she says as her hands travel down my body and grab onto the front of my jeans.

"Darlin', I promise to do whatever you'd like, and I mean whatever you'd like, later at home... in our bed. But right now, I have club business to attend to." I bend, kissing her neck.

"Whatever I like?" she asks, her eyes filled with lust. "I want you to go down on me and make me scream your name. Then, baby, I want you to fuck me hard, and then I want to do it all over again." She smiles at me, and my dick strains to be let out of my jeans.

"Fuck, Kat, you make it hard on a man. I want you right now."

"I could give you a blow job, babe, if you want?"

I raise my eyebrows at her, and I'm about to say yes when I hear, "Hello? Is anyone here?" It's Howie from the café.

Kat laughs, pushes me away, then goes and opens the door. I readjust myself and try to think of something besides her mouth around my cock. I turn around and find Howie looking at Kat as though the sun rises and sets with her.

"Howie." I nod at him and put my arm around Kat's waist, pulling her into me. "How's it going?"

"Good, thanks, Mr. Reynolds. I was dropping off Kat's food," he explains to me as he stares at my woman.

"Yeah, I can see that. How much do I owe you?"

"Oh, it's on the house, Mr. Reynolds. Kat Saunders doesn't pay at Bettie's."

"Howie! How many times have I told you, you have to charge me. If you don't, I'll stop coming. Now, how much do I owe you?" She practically screeches at him. Howie shakes his head, but he has a huge smile on his face. "I mean it, Howie! I'll stop coming!"

"All right, Kat, next time, I promise I'll charge you."

"Howie, I have a witness. Dane will kick your butt if you don't start charging me!" Kat playfully teases him. I smile and shake my head at her antics.

"Yes, Kat, I'm sure he will." As he turns to leave, she slides out of my arms, grabs his upper arm, and kisses him on his cheek.

He goes bright red and trips out the doorway on his way back to the café. "Darlin', you made that boy's day."

"He's sweet, but it's not his day I want to make." She smiles at me seductively and licks her lips.

"Fuck me. Woman, give me Dave's phone number and prepare to be fucked hard tonight. In the meantime, keep away from me, or I'll be using your pretty little mouth in the back room."

Kat laughs and nods as she moves toward her handbag. "I'll send it to you. Now, go, before I take advantage of you."

I give my woman a look, and I have an internal battle raging. I need to have this sorted, but my dick wants some attention. I'm moving toward her when I see Jonas walking across the compound. I go to the front door and whistle. He changes direction and heads toward me.

"Prez, she's nowhere. I have Rebel going through

every storefront, but we can't find her. Emily is gone."

"How can she be gone? Did she buy a ticket and bus it out of town? Where the fuck did she go?" I ask.

"We checked the bus station, and no one matching her description left town today. Martha said there were no strangers, only locals. You know how nosy she can be. You need to confront Agostino. He was the last person we know of who saw her," he says with his arms crossed in front of his chest.

"Who's Emily?" There's more than a hint of frost in Kat's voice. I've never seen my woman jealous before. I think I like it.

"She's my sister, I've mentioned her."

I watch her face as a red blush makes its way up her neck. "Your sister is here? Why didn't you tell me?"

"Darlin', got a lot going on, and I promise tonight we'll go over things, but right now, I need you to stay here. Can you do that for me?" I make it a question, but I don't intend to give her a choice.

"Yes." She moves toward me and wraps her arms around my waist. "You're going to be really busy tonight, and I'll stay here." I kiss the top of her head and move outside with Jonas.

"Brother, that woman is going to be the fucking death of me." He grins at me, knowing what I mean.

"Tell me what you know about Emily's whereabouts."

"Agostino is right. They were in Bettie's Café and then nothing. She left, he had a meal, he left, and that's it. No one has seen her since."

"This day gets fucking worse. I need you to wait out here with me, my brother, while I call Dave. According to Kat, he does background checks on everyone, so if anyone knows fucking anything, it will be him."

He nods, and I check my messages and see the one Kat sent. I call Dave, and he answers on the third ring.

"Dane! How are you? Is my princess all right?"

"How did you know it was me?" I ask.

"Dane, my boy, I have all of your numbers in my phone. Is everything okay?" he repeats himself.

"Your princess is fine. But I have a bit of a situation, and I was wondering if you could help me with some information."

"Dane, my boy, what's my motto? Public perception is the most important thing, and Dave can spin anything! So, hit me with it!" he says flamboyantly.

"It's not that kind of thing, Dave. I need to know about Kat's Ma, Ms. Saunders. What do you know about her?" The line goes quiet, and I say, "Dave, man, you there?"

"I'm here." His voice has gone serious, and there

isn't a trace of humor. "What has she done? What have you found out? Is Kat in any danger?"

"Dave, why would you think Kat is in danger?"

"Her... mother was an interesting person. I assumed because she was involved with you and your... club, you must have known what she was like." There's disdain in his voice.

"Dave, I'm about to come clean with you now, and I need you to keep it to yourself. Do. You. Get. Me?" I pause between every word, letting him know how serious this situation is.

"Of course. I am, after all, a professional."

"Yeah, right. I have only recently discovered Ms. Saunders was into some things that I don't wish to go into over the phone. We never know who's listening. It's come to my attention an associate was helping her and another..." I pause, searching for the right word, "... club but of a different nature is involved. Can you give me anything?"

"I have a file. I'll send it to your personal account at the clubhouse," Dave says.

"Do you need me to give you the address?"

"No need. I have all of your information. I'm sending it now, and I'm coming out. Truth will be with me. He's been having some... issues, and I need to keep an eye on him. So, my boy, do you have room for us, or do I book The Country Inn?"

"There's no fucking need for you to come out, Dave. Kat is safe."

"I need to see it for myself, and it's been weeks since I've seen her. It'll be fun."

"Dave, I know you talk to her every-fucking-day on the phone."

"Fine. Be that way. I've sent the file." He clicks off. Great, I've upset Kat's surrogate father.

I'm standing, scowling at my phone when Jonas asks, "I take it went well?"

"He's sending me a file on Ms. Saunders to my computer at the clubhouse. Go see what it says. I'll deal with Agostino and find out about my sister." I look at Jonas. "What a fucking day!" I growl.

A scream is heard coming from the garage, and we both turn to run toward it as Kat races out and launches herself at me, wrapping her legs around my waist.

"Thank you, baby!" she screams with way too much enthusiasm.

"What the fuck, Kat?" I bellow.

She kisses me on the lips and all over my face, saying repeatedly, "Thank you, thank you, thank you! Dave phoned and said he and Truth are on their way out! I love you!"

With those three words, I'd do anything for her, including putting up with her surrogate overprotective father *and* Truth, her lead guitarist.

Sighing, I put her on the ground. "You know your family is welcome in our home anytime."

"Thank you! Okay, I'm back in the garage. You go

do whatever it is you're doing." She kisses me again and has the biggest smile on her lips as she wanders back inside.

"Well, Dave is a fucker, isn't he? Totally went around you, too, so he could come out here." Jonas laughs, and as I look at him, I laugh, too. Here we are laughing in the lot when Rebel appears before us.

"Did you find her?" asks Rebel. We both stop laughing and look at him. Jonas shakes his head as he wipes tears from his eyes. Rebel looks puzzled at our antics, but he says, "She's nowhere. She left the café then..." he does inverted commas with his hands, "...poof, she's gone."

"Let's go see what Salvatore Agostino has to say about her disappearing. Then we need to talk about Fith. What a fucking day."

We all head for the clubhouse. Inside, my nerves are shot. Fith's running guns for Ms. Saunders. The Abruzzi crime family thinks it's really us. My sister is involved with one of the crime families Captains and now appears to have vanished. Or has she? Or is she in league with him and whatever fucking plans they have cooked up? And now Dave, my wife's gay, over the top father figure, is coming to town with Truth. Truth who talks like a pansy and insists on calling me a *biker*. Can this day get any fucking worse?

Outwardly, for those around me, I project an air

of authority and confidence. I didn't get to be president of this MC by being weak or indecisive.

It took blood and sweat.

And I'd do it all again in a heartbeat to protect what's *mine*.

CHAPTER 24

EMILY

"Amare, a Captain means I'm high up in the Abruzzi family. We're organized. We run most of the East Coast."

"What does it mean, you run most of the East Coast? It sounds like a gang." I can't process what he's saying.

"Not a gang, a family." He reaches across the table and grabs my hands. *"Organized crime, amare. We have a hand in a lot of pies. Not drugs, we're forbidden to become involved in narcotics, but we have a hand in everything else,"* he says it like he was trying to comfort me.

"Guns?" I ask, hoping he doesn't say yes.

"It's the reason I'm here. Your brother is interfering in my business, and we need to know

why." Not only does this man whom I'm attracted to run guns, but my brother does too.

"Guns?" I repeat my question.

"Yes." *Something washes across his features, but I'm unsure what it means.*

"Do you have to sell guns? Could you not do something else?" *I asked, looking for a different answer.*

"I do many other things, it's one of many." *My mind is spinning at his confession. He continued,* "I feel a connection with you, one I have not had with anyone else in a long time. Take some time to think about what you know, and how you feel about me and what I do. For now, let's eat." *Let's eat? There was no way I was going to be able to do it.*

My world is shattered. I tell him I need time to think as I stand and walk out of the café. I head in the direction of the Savage Angels' compound. It's not a long walk, but I'm not sure if I even want to see Dane. Slowing my pace, my mind is swirling with everything that's happened to me in the last few days.

"Excuse me, miss?" A man is beside me.

"Yes?" He stands a little too close to me, making me put some distance between us.

When he holds a map out, I begrudgingly move back toward him. "This is the Main Street in

Tourmaline, yes?"

I smile up at him, as he's easily a foot taller than me. "Yes, you're on Main Street." I move closer and point at his map. "See?"

His arm goes around me, and he says, "Thank you, Emily."

"How do you know—"

He places a cloth over my face, and as I smell a sickly-sweet scent, I feel myself go woozy. "Just breathe, Emily, just breathe."

I feel myself float away.

I'm bent over a table, my arms are stretched out, tied with nylon rope, which goes over the edge of the table, securing me to it. I feel a hand on my back. It goes down my spine and between my legs. I realize I'm naked. Fingers plunge into me, and I scream.

"Good, you're awake. I've been playing with you for a while, but I like it better when you're awake. Please, scream, make a noise. Nothing worse than a woman who lays there and says nothing. You don't have a great rack, but your ass, it's not bad."

My body shudders at the words of my violator.

"Please don't, please!" I scream.

"I'm going to fuck you in every way, in every fucking orifice you have, and I'm going to take my time. That fucker, Sal, should've watched you better."

His hands are on my body, trailing up and down. I feel bile in the back of my throat, and I think I'm going to be sick. He walks in front of me at the head of the table. He takes off his shirt and undoes his belt when his phone rings.

He walks over and grabs it, then comes back and places his hand on my ass and strokes it. "Yeah, boss." He pinches me, and I scream. "Yeah, I have her, she's a screamer." He laughs into his phone. I continue to scream as he slaps my ass. "Hang on, boss, I'll go outside." I stop screaming when I hear the door close.

I'm lying face down on the table with my feet on the floor. Quietly, I wriggle further up it and get my knees under me. He wasn't smart enough to secure my legs. The nylon rope which binds my wrists is looped around the legs of the table. Slowly, I put my feet on the floor at the opposite end and lift one side of the table and then the other. Although the rope is around my wrists, I'm free. I search around for my dress but can't see it. I'm in the kitchen of a very rundown house and the only noise I hear is my attacker on the phone outside. Quietly, I move further into the house, pushing open doors and trying to find something to cover myself. In the last room, at the end of the hallway, there's a smashed window, and I move toward it. Carefully, I poke my head out. I can't see him, and even though I'm naked, I am going to make a run for it. As I step over the sill, I cut my leg on a shard of glass. The pain increases my fear, causing me to fall from the window. Instinctively, I put my hands over my mouth, so I don't scream. I'm lying there for a moment, trying to feel if anything is broken.

"Come out, come out, wherever you are!" sings my attacker.

I can hear doors being flung open, and as he gets closer, I stand and run. The house is in the wilderness, and it looks as though no one has lived here for a long time. I run as fast as I can into the wild, hoping he doesn't follow.

CHAPTER 25

SALVATORE

I have no idea what's going on. The Savage Angels have me sitting at this table without their leader. I drink my third cup of coffee, and I have had enough. I stand, and the one called Kade stands with me. He's wearing a wifebeater, and I can see a tribal tattoo going down one of his arms. He must be six foot three, and clearly built. He carries himself with authority, and at least two of the men around the table follow him. His hair is to his shoulders, and he keeps it tucked behind both ears.

"Am I going to have a sit-down with Reynolds, or are we going to drink coffee all afternoon?" My patience wears thin.

"Dane won't be long. Take a seat and relax." He moves his pale blue eyes to me and his face and voice are void of any emotion.

I straighten my jacket sleeves and do my jacket up. "I don't do business this way. Tell Reynolds to call me when he's ready to sit down. Until then, I'm leaving." I move toward the door, but he stands in my path. I hear chairs scrape across the floor as more of them stand.

"Take a seat," he says and stands up straighter.

"You'll move out of my way. I don't do business with underlings, and I do not take orders from them. Move," I say with a growl.

He stands there, toe to toe with me, and smiles. It doesn't reach his eyes. He steps to the side, and with a sweeping gesture of his arm, he directs me to the door. "By all means, Mr. Agostino, leave. I guess we'll wait for Guido Lamberti and do a deal with him."

I laugh and say, "Yeah, you do that. I can see Guido coming out *here* to do a deal."

His smile increases, and he says, "He's in town. Didn't your Don tell you?"

My laughter stops, and I look at this Kade, who looks pleased to have something over on me. "Guido is here?"

"That's what I said." *Fuck.* I can tell he's not lying.

I stride toward the front door and grab my phone out of my jacket. I hit call as Reynolds makes it to me from across the lot. I hold up my finger in his face and wait for Tony to answer.

"Yeah, boss."

"Tony, Guido is here in this little fucking town." I look at Reynolds and say, "Tell me, did you know he was here."

"Boss, of course not!" Tony says.

I hold a finger up at Reynolds, indicating for him to be quiet again, and he scowls at me. "Tony, I wasn't talking to you. Send my best men and have them come here. I'll need at least six men. Do it now."

"On it, boss, you want me there?"

"Yeah, Tony, I said my best men."

I hang up and stare at Reynolds, who says, "You sure you're fucking *done*? Can I fucking speak now in my *own* fucking compound?"

My hands are up, trying to placate a very aggressive Dane Reynolds. "I apologize. I meant no disrespect. Why didn't you tell me Guido Lamberti was here?"

"He's one of yours. Why didn't you know?" he counters.

"What the fuck is going on? Why are you running guns on the East Coast? We had a fucking deal!" I throw my hands up in frustration and pace.

"Jonas, give us a minute, yeah?" Reynolds looks at his man, who nods and walks toward the clubhouse. "I didn't know you had a deal with Ms. Saunders. I had no idea she was running guns, and we were the security for it. I don't know about your deal. We don't run illegal activities of any-fucking-kind out of Tourmaline." He finally lifts his eyes to mine, and he looks defeated.

"You didn't know? Then how the fuck did you manage to muscle in on my territory, not to mention, Don Abruzzi has not been paid a tribute!" I can feel my blood boil. My rage simmers on the surface, waiting for something to trigger it.

"Ms. Saunders wasn't who we fucking thought she was. I have someone coming in tomorrow who may be able to answer some questions about her, and I have one of my guys running a background check. We ran security on her runs because we thought we were protecting Carnival-fucking-Cigarettes. Not guns. It appears as though one of my guys knew about her and kept it going after she died. I'm guessing he was the one who expanded her business. He didn't fucking know about you or your family."

I nod my head, trying to understand what he's saying. It makes sense they wouldn't run guns out of where they live. Ms. Saunders was devious, but these aren't choirboys but a large organization, and I'd think, not easily fooled.

"Why didn't you run a check previously? She had many deals with many people. Her dealings are far and wide. I know with her death, there were some wars as the gangs tried to gain control of her share."

"We thought she was a little old lady who owned

a transport business. I kid you not, she cooked muffins for us, came to my home every Sunday and cooked breakfast for us, and we took her shopping. I had *no* fucking idea."

He's being completely honest with me. This isn't something I expected. From the little information I could gather on him, I know he is loyal to his MC and, more recently, his woman, Kat Saunders, lead singer of The Grinders. He's a simple man who runs his organization with an iron fist. This will reflect badly on him if this all goes sideways.

Time to lay all my cards on the table. "I was sent here by Don Abruzzi. He got his enforcer, Guido, to tell me to come here alone and fix this. I'm a Captain in the family, and it's unusual for someone in my position to have to deal with this." I make a sweeping gesture with my arm. "Your sister, Emily, did you plant her in my path on purpose?"

"Man, I didn't know either of you were coming. Have you got her stashed somewhere?"

"No, I don't have her." I pause and look at him, trying to see if there's truth in his words. "If Guido is here, the Don must be upset with me. Guido is here for one reason only, and that will be to take me out if this goes south." I place one hand on my hip and rub my face with the other while pondering everything I've learned.

"Did your Don tell you personally?" he asks

I look at him and shake my head. "What? No, he

went through Guido."

Rebel walks toward us, and neither one of us say anything as we watch him approach. "Prez." He nods at me. "Do we know where Emily is?"

"You're serious? She's not here?" My gut churns with this realization.

Rebel says, "No, she disappeared after she left the café. No one saw where she went. Rosie said you stayed in the café and finished your meal, so I know it wasn't you."

"What do you mean, it wasn't me?" I ask, anger coming back to the surface. I look at Reynolds, and his face is a mask of concern.

"She didn't get a bus out of town, she's not in any of the shops or the Doc's or even the fucking motel. As far as we know, she only knows *you* and Addy. Has to be a snatch and grab."

Rebel's words sink in, and my mind goes to Guido. Could Guido have done this to use her as a bargaining tool? She'd be easy to grab, she's tiny, and I'm not sure if she has it in her to fight back.

My gaze goes to Reynolds. "I didn't do this. If she has been taken, it wasn't by me. But Guido? He may be using her to get to you or me."

Reynolds' look goes from concerned to rage, and he snarls at me. "Where would he fucking take her?"

"Be calm. I'll find out if it's the last thing I do," I say, trying to reassure him.

"No, this is my town, and I've had enough of being kept in the fucking dark. I'm going to get that fucker Guido and his fucking sidekick and bring them here. I'll skin him alive if he's hurt her. You'll stay here," he says as he pushes me toward the clubhouse.

This man isn't in my family. He has no authority over me and does not get to push me. I stand my ground and step into his space. Normally, I'd not openly challenge someone on their home turf, but I've had enough.

I'm about to punch him when I hear, "Hello! I'm Kat Saunders, and that's my man you're about to tangle with." We both turn and stare at her. She holds up both hands and continues, "I have no idea what's going on—"

"Kat, go back into the garage." Reynolds snarls at her.

Then she puts her hands on her hips and laughs. She laughs so hard she doubles over. I look at Reynolds and raise an eyebrow, and he shakes his head from side to side, signaling he has no idea what she's doing.

When she's finally under control, she says, "Go back to the garage? You're kidding, right?" She grabs each of us by the elbow and walks us toward the clubhouse. She laughs to herself as she says, "I don't know what's going on. I don't care, not really, but if you think for one minute, I'm going to stand there and watch you two duke it out... oh my God, you have another thing coming. So, let's go have a stiff drink and talk this out like the adults we are. Oh, and, baby, you know the deal we have going for tonight... well, I'm thinking if you think you can order me around like a dog, then I'm not interested."

I glance at Reynolds, and he looks pained. Whatever their deal is, he isn't happy it's canceled. She lets us go and pushes the doors of the clubhouse open.

The tension between us has dissipated. "She's a strong woman, you're lucky."

"You have no fucking idea."

I watch as she walks up to the bar and orders three whiskeys. She has a nice ass. I stare at it, then Reynolds clears his throat, and I look at him.

"Is there anything we should know about Guido?"

"He'll be armed. You're best to offer him an invitation but make it so he can't refuse, escort him here, and don't let him or any of his men out of your sight."

He nods as his woman places a shot of whiskey in his hands and then mine. She looks from one of us to the other, holds hers up, and says, "To new friends, may we know each other for a long and happy time!" She throws hers back, does a little dance. and then throws her arms in the air and says,

"Woo-hoo!"

I look at Reynolds, who smiles, then we both laugh.

"That's better! Now, I'm taking myself back to the garage, but I'd appreciate it if someone took me home. I'm bored, and I've had enough. Shall I give you, say, one more hour?" she asks as she stares Reynolds in the eye.

"I'd appreciate it if you stayed here in the compound. You don't have to stay in the garage. But, darlin', I need you to stay in the compound."

She flips her long hair over her shoulder and stalks out of the clubhouse. Reynolds looks at the ceiling and swears. I laugh.

Kat Saunders is one feisty woman.

He looks at me. "I'll deal with Kat later, but let's go back to my sister. Do you think Guido has her?"

"No. He'd have phoned you by now. If he's trying to use her as a bargaining tool, you'd know about it. She's probably sitting somewhere, taking stock of her situation. Are there any parks or somewhere she could be sitting where your men may have missed?" I'm not really concerned. If they did have Emily, they would've made contact. Reynolds is wise to keep his woman safe here in the compound, even if she doesn't like it.

Rebel comes through the clubhouse doors. "Prez, what are we doing about Emily?" he asks.

"Sal thinks she could be somewhere taking

things in, he—"

"Really? I've looked all over Tourmaline. I've questioned everyone who was on the street when she left the café, and lots of people remember her leaving, but then nothing. You don't find it strange? It's a small town, you don't think someone would know where she is?" he says, pinning me with a look.

"I can see your point, but if Guido had her, he'd have called by now," I reply.

"Well, maybe it's not Guido, maybe it's someone else." Rebel looks at his president. "I want to ask Sheriff Morales if he'll get Mr. Finlay from the hardware store to show us his video footage. He wouldn't show it to me, thinks we're all thugs."

Reynolds nods at him. "Can't hurt. Go see Morales."

Before Reynolds has even finished his sentence, Rebel heads for the front doors. Perhaps I'm wrong? She seems to have a knack for getting herself into trouble. I feel uneasy. Rebel is right, it might not be Guido. It hadn't occurred to me someone else might have taken her.

Reynolds looks at me. "I'm going back in there to ask my boys to look for Emily. Our business will have to wait."

I nod at him. "I can wait. Your sister should take priority, but you need to handle Guido. Perhaps I could help?"

He straightens up and squares his shoulders. "You fuck me over on this in any way, and you're dead. You get me?"

A lazy smile plays on my lips. "Yeah, I get you. I'll not screw you over, you have my word." Reynolds stands there for a heartbeat, sizing me up, then nods and walks off in search of his men.

CHAPTER 26

EMILY

I run blindly through the trees, and my feet have been cut on rocks and branches because of it. My arms are all scraped up from the many times I have fallen. I'm so scared. I have no idea how long I've been running, and I'm trying to go straight—I read in a book we tend to walk in a circle, so I'm trying not to do it. I keep picking landmarks ahead of me and run toward them. I stop and take a breather and listen. I can't hear anyone calling out for me, and I can't hear anyone in pursuit. The nylon rope has cut into my wrists, so I look around and notice there's a boulder near me. I need to figure out a way to cut the rope. Using a sharp edge, I try to rub the rope on it in hopes it's enough to sever my binds.

Come on, Em, you can do this. I keep rubbing

away, but I'm taking more skin off than cutting the rope. *Okay, time to stop. It's not working, and I'm doing myself more damage. Where am I? He's obviously not pursuing me.*

Crouching down, I cry. My body hurts everywhere. I look at my leg, and there's blood running down it from the cut caused by the window. I have no way to stop it, nevertheless, I wipe it with my hands and see it's a deep gash, but not serious. If I were in town, I'd probably have stitches. I sigh and look around. All I can see are trees. I need to find civilization. I need to find a road or someone to help me.

I don't understand why that man would do what he did to me, and I shudder as I think of what he wanted to do. There's an ache between my legs. My tears flow more freely, and I sob, making huge wailing noises. I put my hands over my mouth to try to stop them or at least cover the noise. Falling to my knees, I try to take in deep breaths to calm down. I stand and stare at my surroundings. I think there are only a few hours of daylight left. Although I've never camped in the wild before, I have watched many survival shows, and if I don't find shelter or a way out, I could die out here from exposure.

There are mountains up ahead in the distance. If I move toward them, hopefully, I'll find a cave or something to protect me from the elements. I've

seen how to make a fire, but I have never tried it.
   I sigh and begin my trek toward the mountains.

CHAPTER 27

SHERIFF CARLOS MORALES

Rebel, a member of the Savage Angels, has walked into my station and asked to speak to me. I stand in the doorway of my office and motion for him to come to me. He's wearing his cut and looks serious. I have a tenuous relationship with the Savage Angels. If it weren't for Kat Saunders, I wouldn't have one at all.

When that psycho, Gareth Goodman, killed Jess Cliffe in Kat's home, I became entangled in their world. Goodman's trial is finally coming, and I have to testify against him. He's tried every trick in the book to either have his trial thrown out or postponed, but next month, it goes ahead. The courts have decided he's of sound mind, and hopefully, he'll receive the death penalty, but he has a huge following, so finding an impartial jury could be hard.

"Sheriff, can I speak to you privately?" asks Rebel, bringing me out of my thoughts.

"Sure, Reb, take a seat. What can I do for you?" I go around my desk and take a seat facing him.

"Sheriff, Dane's sister, Emily, came to town a couple of days ago, and now she's disappeared. She was seen leaving Bettie's today, then nothing."

"What do you need me for, Rebel?" I say, leaning forward on my desk.

"Sheriff, Mr. Finlay at the hardware store has a camera facing the street. He might have footage of where she went, but he won't let me see it. I was hoping you could convince him."

"Let's go for a walk, Rebel, and you can tell me all about Emily and how she came to be here, yes?" I grab my gun out of my drawer, pick up my hat, and head for the front of the station. Deputy Bill Barrett, who I have long suspected is in partnership with the Savage Angels, looks up from his desk. "Barrett, I need you to come with me. We're headed into town. Get your equipment."

"Yes, Sheriff. I'm on it,"

I give him a stiff smile and head outside, Rebel right beside me. "Do you think something bad has happened to this woman?"

"I don't know, Sheriff, all I know is she was supposed to come and see Dane, and she didn't. I've searched everywhere, and after she left Bettie's, no one saw her. Either she didn't talk to any of the locals, or she's been taken." I look at Rebel, and he has genuine concern on his face.

"I saw her this morning outside Doc Jordan's, and she looked kind of beat up. You know anything about it?" I ask.

"She'd been in a car accident. About four hours from here. She got a ride into town with Salvatore Agostino." He says the man's name with disgust, as though he doesn't like him.

"Something I should know about him?"

"No, Sheriff, he hasn't done anything. It's a feeling and nothing I care to share."

"Fair enough." I stare at him, and then Deputy Barrett joins us. "Let's go to the hardware store, shall we?"

We walk three abreast down Main Street. Those who are on the street stop and stare. I'm sure they think Rebel has done something wrong. I nod as we pass them and receive general greetings from some.

The women openly stare at me. I'm considered a catch here in Tourmaline. The female population probably knows everything about me, and at times, it can be a problem. I can't really date anyone in town because if it goes south, they tend to tell their girlfriends, and it spreads like wildfire. I like Adelynn at The Country Inn, but she's hooked on one of the Savage Angels. Occasionally, we go out for company, or when I realize the local female population is paying me too much attention.

As we hit the front entrance of the hardware store, Mr. Finlay comes to meet us. "Sheriff, Deputy." He nods at us, completely ignoring Rebel.

"Mr. Finlay, we were wondering if we could take a look at your camera footage from earlier today."

"Of course, Sheriff, anything for Tourmaline's finest." He smiles at us, then heads toward the back of the store.

I look at Rebel, smile, and raise my eyebrows. He shakes his head, and we all follow Finlay.

"I have it all cued up, Sheriff, to the time this ruffian said the girl disappeared. Haven't looked at it yet, was about to," says Mr. Finlay as he stares at me, trying to pretend Rebel isn't giving him a death stare.

"It's very good of you, Mr. Finlay. Would you mind leaving us while we view the footage, police business, you know?" I smile at him and grab the door to his office. He walks out, and as he turns around to say something, I shut the door. "Ok, Deputy, hit play."

He glances at Rebel, then takes a seat behind the desk and hits play on the recorder. Rebel and I stand close together and watch the screen as we see a female come into view.

"That's her," says Rebel. Then we see a man

holding out a piece of paper. She steps closer to him. It appears as though they exchange a few words, and then her body seems to sag. He keeps her upright, and they move out of sight.

"Rewind it and play it again," I order. Barrett does as he's told, and we watch it again. "It looks like he's carrying her at the end, but I can't be sure." I look over at Rebel. "Does he look familiar?"

He shakes his head and says, "No, but maybe Agostino knows him?"

I nod. I'd forgotten about him. He has to be tied up in this somehow. "Why is he here, Rebel?" I ask, knowing he probably won't tell me.

"He has business with the club, and he brought Emily to town. He must know more than he's letting on. How about you go question him, Sheriff?"

"How about I go question him? You don't want this done in-house?" I ask, incredulous he'd want an outsider brought in.

"No, Sheriff, I want her found. I've spent time with her, Carlos. She had no idea who we were, and she trusted us immediately. Most people fear us or hate us, but no one trusts us straightaway."

He's trying to build a relationship with me by using my name, and it makes me stop and think. "Okay, Rebel, is Agostino staying at The Country Inn?" I ask, and he nods. I look at Deputy Barrett. "Go check out the motel, check his car, and speak to Adelynn or her father. Get a feel for him and get back to me on my phone. Got it?"

"Yes, Sheriff!" And like the good little soldier he pretends to be, he rushes out of the hardware store.

I look at Rebel. "Grab the tape, and let's take a walk to see your boss, sorry... prez. Isn't that what you call him?"

"Carlos, you know damn well he's our president. Stop being a dick."

I nod at him. "It's Sheriff, Rebel, and yeah, I know he's your president." He grabs the tape, and we head to the front of the store.

On the way out, Rebel stops in front of Mr. Finlay. "Wanted to say thank you for letting us take this." He waves it around in front of him. "We really appreciate your cooperation." It looks as though Mr. Finlay is about to explode. His face is bright red, but all he does is nod. He doesn't make eye contact, and Rebel walks out with no further confrontation, thankfully.

We walk together toward the compound, neither of us speaking. When we arrive at the gates, I see Agostino climb into a car, so I walk toward it with my hand on my hip. I stand at the window and tap on it, and he winds it down.

"Got a few questions for you, so I need you to climb out of the car, Mr. Agostino."

"I'm on my way out. When we come back, yes?"

"No, I don't want to have to ask again but get out of the car, Mr. Agostino." I open the door and stand there, hand on hip.

He looks straight ahead, then nods at the driver and slowly steps out. "As you wish, Sheriff." He straightens his jacket and says, "Shall we go inside?"

I nod at him and motion for him to go first. He smiles and leads the way. "Thank you for your compliance, Mr. Agostino."

"I remember you, Sheriff, but you weren't a sheriff back then, you were Detective Morales, as I recall." He looks at me and smiles.

I wondered how long it would take him to remember me. Working in New Jersey, I got to see the scum of the earth. There are a lot of good people there, but in the end, I couldn't distinguish the good from the bad. It turned me into someone I don't care to remember. When I got this job, it was a lifeline, a way to start again, a way to forget my past.

I smile and lean into him, hand still on my hip. "Yes, that's right, I was a detective, but now, Mr. Agostino, I'm Sheriff Morales, and I expect you to answer a few questions."

He looks at my hand on my gun, smiles, and continues toward the clubhouse doors. "I'll answer your questions, Sheriff, but you should know Guido Lamberti is in town."

Fuck, Guido Lamberti?

The fucker is a stone-cold killer. I could never find anything to stick to him. When I had witnesses, they either ended up dead or were paid off and still ended up dead. My obsession with him cost me everything, and now he's here in Tourmaline. I look at Agostino, and he smiles knowingly. I want to punch those very straight white teeth down his throat. He shrugs at me, and I grab him by his nicely tailored jacket and move him backward with everything I have. I don't stop until his body crashes into the outside wall of the clubhouse, then the Savage Angels pull me off him.

I roar, "*Get your fucking hands off me!*" They all retreat, and I stand there, taking in gulps of air, trying to control my rage. Agostino looks incensed. I bet it's been a long time since anyone has dared lay hands on him. I turn away from him, unable to even look at him and have him remind me of the person I was. I've worked too fucking hard to create a life here, to have friends, to belong to a community. Then my phone rings. I absently grab it from my pocket and say in a loud voice, "What?"

"Sheriff? Is that you?"

"Yes, who the fuck do you think it is?" I know it's Deputy Barrett on the other end of the line, and I know I'm taking my anger out on him, but at the moment, I don't give a fuck.

"Sorry, sir... ahh... Sheriff. I did what you said. I spoke to Addy at The Country Inn, and I looked in his room. But, Sheriff, there's blood on the seat in his car."

I hold my phone away from my ear and slowly turn around. My hand is still on my gun, and I pull it out of the holster. I hear shouts around me as I point it at Agostino.

"You're coming with me to the station to answer a few questions. Now move!"

Agostino fixes his jacket and says, "Calm down, Sheriff, I'm coming. No need to point your gun at me."

Rebel walks up to me, hands in the air. "Sheriff? I thought we were going to talk to Agostino, show him the tape."

I glance at Rebel and nod. I slowly put my gun in its holster. "You're right, Rebel, but we're doing it back at the station. New evidence has come to light."

"Fresh evidence?" he asks, then he turns to Agostino, and this time, he grabs him and pushes him up against the wall. "What have you done?"

I place my hand on Rebel's shoulder. "Help me transport him back to the station, Rebel."

"That's not going to be necessary, Sheriff. If Agostino knows anything, we'll find out," says a very disgruntled Dane Reynolds.

"Afraid I can't let you do that, Dane, and you know it. Seeing as she's your sister, I'll allow you to observe the interview, but you can't take part in it. Understood?"

"Think I liked you better when you had your gun

out, Sheriff," Reynolds retorted.

I scoff at him and nod. "A moment of... madness. Let's go, Agostino." I grab him by the arm and walk him out of the compound.

CHAPTER 28

JOHNNIE

Fucking little cunt got away from me! Guido will not be pleased. I didn't even get to fuck her. I hold my fingers up to my nose. I can still smell her scent, and my cock is so fucking hard. She ran off into the wilderness, and there's no way I'm going after her. I know nothing about the wild. With any luck, she'll fall and break her neck. My biggest problem is telling Guido. I've been in his employ for over ten years, but this is a major fuck-up. I'm not sure what he's going to do. No good putting it off any longer, so I dial his number. It's been about an hour since she disappeared, and I can't see her anywhere. It's time to confess.

"Johnnie?"

"Hey, boss."

He laughs. "You finished with her already? You need to learn how to drag things out, savor the moment, you know?"

"Boss, she escaped." I'm greeted with silence at the end of the line. I wait a moment, then say, "Boss? You there?"

"Yes, I'm here." Then more silence.

"It happened while I was on the phone with you. I tried to find her, but she's run off into the woods. There's not another home around for miles, and she's naked. With any luck, she's broken her neck or something."

"That was over an hour ago." His voice has gone steely. I've heard this tone before, but normally, it's before he tells me to kill someone. "What the fuck took you so long to tell me!"

"I was trying to find her, boss. I'm sorry. I know I've fucked up. What do you want me to do?"

I hear him sigh. "All right, stay where you are. She might come back. I think the Savage Angels have made us anyway, so we might need you later. Johnnie, I'm not pleased." He clicks off.

Fuck! Guido isn't pleased. I'm not sure how I am going to make it up to him, but I will. In the meantime, I'm going to relieve myself while smelling my fingers. Shouldn't take long.

CHAPTER 29

EMILY

I've built a fire, and I think I have it sheltered from the direction I ran from. I used the fire to melt the nylon rope off myself, burning my wrists in the process. My poor hands have blisters on the palms from making the fire, and the sides of them have scrapes from my previous attempt to remove the rope.

There's enough underbrush on the ground so no one could sneak up on me. I used a reasonably flat piece of wood to smooth out somewhere to lie down, and I've placed leaves there, so I'm not too uncomfortable. My biggest concern is dehydration. If I remember correctly, it's what gets you first, so I'm trying to conserve my energy. I even sharpened a stick on a boulder and now have a pretty mean-looking stake. I'm not going down without a fight, not this time.

When Dane left all those years ago, our father got worse for a time, but only with our mother and not with me. My torment didn't start until I got my first period. It was the first time he hit me—I was only thirteen. I remember my mother putting herself between us and shaking her head violently from side to side. I didn't understand, but later I would.

He tried to touch me a few times, but my mother went after him in a way I'd never seen her do before.

She never stood up to him, so it came as a complete surprise. It broke something in him. For a time, he stopped drinking, stopped being a bully, and we were like a normal family. I even had friends, which was something I never had before. My mother never let him be alone with me, ever. Even when he wasn't drinking, she was always vigilant.

I was twenty and away at college when she was killed. I went home for the funeral, and I remember he reeked of alcohol as I stood beside him, holding my hand. My mother was proud of me when I went off to school. I had to work two jobs to be able to afford to go, but she told me never to come back, not even for holidays. She'd occasionally come up and visit, but it was always alone. I know my father thought he loved her, but it wasn't really love. He wanted to possess her, to own her, and to control everything she did. I think she thought she didn't have a way out, so she stayed. I think they were happy before she died. Ma had resigned herself to a life with him and made the best of it.

I got my first phone call from the local police station about twelve months after she passed. Dad had been picked up trying to put his car keys into the ignition of his car but was so drunk he couldn't find the right key. They had him in a drunk tank, but technically, he hadn't done anything wrong. If only they had let him drive and then picked him up. So, I went home for a week, threw out all his bottles, paid his bills, and almost wiped out my bank account doing it.

The next time was about six months later, then the calls became more and more frequent until he was diagnosed with cancer. In the end, I'd missed so much school, I deferred for twelve months, but I never went back. I got a job in a local call center and tried to make enough money to pay to maintain the house. I even worked nights for a while, but I couldn't continue that for long—the lack of sleep wasn't good for me.

He'd be good for a while, then he'd start drinking again. We were lucky he was a functioning alcoholic. He had a good health plan with his work, and they paid a lot of the medical bills, but not all. I still have a huge debt where that's concerned. He only tried to hit me a couple of times, but I made it clear I'd leave.

He was fine during the days, apologetic even. I always wondered what happened to him to make him so angry, so miserable, and so hateful.

My bedroom became my safe haven. I put locks on my bedroom door, so he couldn't come into my room when I was asleep. The nights were the worst. I'd sleep with a knife under my pillow and push my chest of drawers in front of the door.

I was lucky I had my own bathroom since my ma insisted I have one. I think even all those years ago, she knew what he was capable of and didn't want to put me in any kind of danger. She tried her best.

If I have children, there's no way I could do what she did. She should've left, and I often wonder why she didn't.

It was like I had become the parent and he the child. He was so angry at the end. He didn't want to die. He told me this many times with tears running down his face. He picked at and belittled everything I did, even when I was trying to help. I had a nurse come to the house once a day to wash him and see to him, but in the end, he didn't even want to shower. It wore him out. Once, I accidentally gave him too much morphine, he was in so much pain, and he hallucinated. I called the ambulance. It's my fondest memory of him—he was happy. He told me my mother was there with us—he was smiling and talking to her. When the ambulance arrived, they took him to the palliative care unit in our local hospital. He lasted three more days. He was nice to me, told me he loved me, and this is how I'm going to try to remember him. I want to forget the hateful bastard who dominated so much of my life.

The light is fading and with it, I push all memories of my father to the back of my mind. I pray someone is looking for me. Throwing another log on the fire, I stare into it. I never thought I'd be lost in the woods, naked. The reunion with my brother is nothing like I thought it would be. Right now, I'm wishing I took that doctor up on his offer instead of being hurt and scared in the middle of nowhere.

Lord, please send someone to help me.

CHAPTER 30

SALVATORE

I sit in an interrogation room. It isn't the first one I have been in and probably won't be the last. It doesn't intimidate me. I drum my fingers on the desktop and stare at the mirror. The door to the room opens, and a deputy rolls in a television and VCR, plugs them in, and leaves.

Sheriff Morales enters the room. He places a tape in the VCR, turns the television on, hits play, and then sits opposite me. I stare at the television, boredom plastered across my features. Then I see Emily on the screen—I know it's her from the dress—a man approaches her, and I see her move toward him. She seems to fall into him, but I can't be sure. Then they move out of the shot. I glare at the sheriff, stand up, and rewind the tape, then watch it again, this time paying more attention to the man.

"It looks like Johnnie Vanetti. He's one of Guido's men. I can't be sure, but it looks like him," I say.

"Can you tell me how you got blood in your car?" asks the Sheriff.

I sigh and give the Sheriff my full attention. "When I met Emily, she'd been in a car accident. She hit her head on the steering wheel, and she had a cut above her eye. Your local doctor even attended to her, you could ask him. She got blood on my seats from her head wound. She offered to have my seats cleaned. I can assure you I had nothing to do with her disappearance. But you know this already, don't you, Sheriff?"

"Why is Guido Lamberti here?"

"This I don't know. I was on my way to see him when you picked me up. The Savage Angels should have him by now, perhaps when they bring him to Tourmaline, you can ask him." I understand how hard it is for this man. From the little I knew of him, he pursued Guido vigorously, but we had the money and the resources that he did not, and it didn't help his partner was on the take. He was never going to win.

He looks at me, stands, and leaves the room. Rubbing hands over my face, I stand and pace, trying to understand what the fuck is going on.

I knock on the glass. "I need my phone, or I need

to use a phone." I stare at my reflection and say, "Now." I continue to stare at myself, then sit back down. Moments later, a deputy comes into the room with my phone. "Thank you." He smiles at me and then leaves.

I dial Don Abruzzi at home. It's answered on the fifth ring by a female. "Hello!" She sounds overly bright and bubbly.

"Hello, this is Salvatore Agostino, is Don Abruzzi available?"

"Sal! It's Lexi! How the hell are you?" Lexi Mancini, one of the Don's granddaughters, asks.

"I'm well, Lexi, and you?"

"Oh, you know, same old, same old. How long's it been, one... no... two years?" she asks.

"I believe it's been two years. Lexi, I need to speak to your grandfather. Is he there?" I ask, trying to sound casual.

"No, Sal, he's gone out to buy cannoli as no one would make it for him. Do you want me to get him to call you when he comes back?"

"Yes, please. Now, I hate to rush off, but I must get back to business Take care, yes?"

"Yes, Sal, take care!" she says as she hangs up. Lexi Mancini is a party girl. I'm sure she'll one day put her grandfather into an early grave. I hope she at least remembers I've called.

The door to the interrogation room opens, and a deputy stands in the doorway. "You can go now, Mr.

Agostino, but please don't leave town."

I smile at him and say, "Of course, deputy. I'll be at The Country Inn if you're looking for me." I walk out of the room and out of the station. I don't stop to see if anyone is following me and make my way toward the motel.

"Sal!" I stop and turn to face Reynolds as he jogs to catch up with me. When he comes close enough, I raise my eyebrows at him. "I know it couldn't have been pleasant to have been in that fucking room but come on, man, you know he had to fucking question you."

"Really? He could've showed me the fucking footage of Emily being taken by Johnnie Vanetti, and we could all be out looking for her. Tell me, Dane, did he tell you Johnnie did a stretch for rape? Did he tell you about the countless other charges which have been brought against him, but the witnesses disappear?" I can tell by the look on his face the sheriff has not, so I continue, "No? Yes, that's the type of man who has your sister, and if she's still alive, she'll wish she wasn't." I turn my back on him and head toward the motel again. Rage clouds my thoughts. It makes no sense for them to have taken her and not to have phoned. Too much risk if they just wanted a fuck. I arrive at my car and climb in. The passenger door opens, and Reynolds climbs in uninvited.

"The Sheriff didn't tell me fucking jack about

Vanetti. Guido is on his way to the compound. We'll only have a brief window before the Sheriff arrives. What's your plan?" he says.

"My plan is to meet Guido before he gets to your compound and confront him before the Sheriff arrives," I grind out.

"That's what I thought, so I'm coming with you."

Turning to him, I nod and start the car. I reverse out of the parking stall, then I put it in gear, and we're on the road heading toward Guido.

"Let me do the talking. Guido is someone I have had dealings with in the past. He's not to be fucked with, and you don't want to put all your cards out on the table. Understand?" I glance at him, and he nods. "Good."

CHAPTER 31

GUIDO

A car and half a dozen motorbikes pull up in the parking lot of the motel. I stare out the window through the sheer curtains, looking at them all. It's an impressive sight. They're all in their colors. Some dismount while others stay astride their bikes, waiting for orders. I watch them as they go into the manager's office, presumably to find out where we are. As they leave it, one of them signals to two of the others, and then he points to my door. Four of them head my way, and then one of them pounds on the door. I smile—time for negotiations.

As I swing open the door, they step back. "Good evening..." I pause and look at them, "... gentlemen." Then I chuckle. "What can I do for you?" My contempt is obvious, and these bikers have no fucking idea who they're dealing with.

"Mr. Lamberti, your presence is required at our clubhouse in Tourmaline, if you'll come with us?" says one of them, and his level of respect is evident. It takes me by surprise.

"Of course, but you are?" He's easily six foot six, with light green eyes, and if I had to judge his age, I'd say thirty. His hair is long, and he has a part of it pulled back off his face.

"I'm Jonas Quinn, VP of the Savage Angels. We'd appreciate it if you and your associate would get into the car." He makes it so I can't decline. Although he's respectful, his tone is of one who's used to being in charge.

"You're only the VP?" I step outside and look around. "Surely, for someone of my stature, I deserve the man in charge?" I glance to my right and see Vinnie has stepped out. He moves to step toward me and raises his eyebrows. I smile at him and nod. He knows by my demeanor not to panic.

"No disrespect is meant. Our president is waiting for you in Tourmaline. Please get into the car." This time, it's more forceful. I shrug and slowly make my way to the car.

Vinnie climbs in one side and I on the other. They have not patted us down for guns, which I find interesting. There's no way in my world we'd not have done that.

Amateurs.

No wonder I haven't had dealings with them before now.

This Jonas Quinn hands over his motorcycle keys to one of his men, and I hear him say, "You scratch my bitch even a little bit, and you'll be paying for a new coat of paint." Then he smiles and pats the man on the shoulder.

When he enters the car, he says, "You may be wondering why we didn't take your weapons. It's a sign of respect, but, Mr. Lamberti, if you or your associate misbehave, we'll fuck you up." Then he smiles at me and buckles up his seat belt. This one has balls.

"We will behave. Now, take us to your leader." My laughter fills the air, and like the good soldier Vinnie is, he joins in.

CHAPTER 32

DANE

The drive to Pearl County is done in silence. I know I told Salvatore I'd let him handle Guido Lamberti, but if he has my sister, that will be a different matter. At the moment, it's better to work with him than against him.

By the time we reach the convoy coming from Pearl, night is falling. Whoever has Emily has had her for hours. My only hope is they keep her safe and think she's valuable to Salvatore or me.

The car has barely come to a stop when I'm out and pull open the door to grab Guido Lamberti. I have him by the shirt and pushed up against the side of the car when I realize his soldier has a gun pointed at me.

"You will take your hands off of Mr. Lamberti, or

I'll shoot you," says the man inside the car.

"You take the fucking gun off me, and I might let you fucking live. How does that sound?" I growl at him. He cocks the gun, and Jonas sticks his own Glock in the guy's face.

"Vinnie, is it? This is the man in charge, our president. Now, if you don't put your gun away, I'm going to put a very big fucking hole in your head."

Now that Jonas has him under control, I look at the man I want so badly to beat, but he isn't looking at me.

I feel a hand on my shoulder, and I hear, "This isn't the way, Dane, you'll get nothing out of him this way. We must show Mr. Lamberti the correct amount of respect. This is how it's done."

Guido laughs, and I can feel the vein in my neck pulse.

"I tell you what? This fucker tells me where Emily is, and I let him live. This is how we do it," I say.

Guido locks his eyes with mine. "Emily? Who's Emily? I'm here to find out why you have undercut the Abruzzi family business and to find out how much you cut Sal, here, in for." He smiles, and I can see he's a fucking liar.

I straighten out his shirt and pat him on the shoulders, then take a step back and smile. He smiles at me.

"Get his man out of the car." I reach into Guido's

jacket, pull out his gun, and smile at him. "Pat them both down and make sure no one has any weapons."

Guido cocks his head to the side and stares at me as Jonas pats him down.

When he's flipped over, I glance at Salvatore. "If the situation were reversed, and she was your sister, would you react any differently?" I ask.

"Dane, I think I know your sister better than you, so yes, I *would*, and I*'m* reacting differently to you. This isn't the way," he repeats.

"So, the sister means something to you, Sal? Apparently, you two are very cozy. How come we haven't seen her before? Where have you been hiding her?" asks Guido.

"Guido, I promise you I only met this woman a few days ago. Return her to her family before it's too late," Salvatore appeals to Guido.

"You expect me to believe that? A man doesn't shower a stranger in gifts unless, of course, she's a good fuck, so tell me, Sal, is she? Or do I have to wait to ask Johnnie?" Guido laughs, and so does his man.

Red colors my vision as I punch him in the mouth and feel his teeth loosen. I pull back to hit him again when Sal grabs my arm.

"There are too many witnesses. We're out in the open. This needs to be done in private," he says in a whisper, so only Guido and I can hear.

"Take your fucking hands off me." I snarl at Sal.

He releases my arm, and I watch as Guido spits two of his teeth into the dirt. I smile. "Get them both back into the car. We'll take them to the old mill out past town. I want everyone out there. Spread the word." I look at Sal. "Let's go, Sal." I stride away and get into the driver's seat of his car. Once inside, I call Kat.

She answers the phone with, "I'm still mad at you."

"I know, and I deserve it. Kat, I need you to—"

"Dane, everyone is leaving. What's going on?" she asks.

"Darlin', I need you to go to Bettie's Café. Ask one of the boys to escort you there before they all leave town. I don't have time to tell you everything, but I will in due time, okay?"

Surprisingly, she doesn't argue with me. "All right, Bettie's closes at nine. Will you be back by then, and... are you safe?"

Her question takes me by surprise. "Yes, darlin', I'm safe." Sal climbs into the car. "If I am not back by ten to nine, call the sheriff and ask him to drive you home and ask him to do a walk through before he leaves, then set the alarm. Don't open the door to anyone but a brother. Is that clear?"

"Yes, Dane. I love you." As always, it amazes me she could say and mean those words to me.

I close my eyes and say, "Later." I hang up, replaying her words over and over in my mind.

"What the fuck was that?" Sal says.

"What the fuck was what?" I say, staring at him.

"I asked you to let me handle the negotiations, and you went and did that. How the fuck am I going to salvage what you have done?"

"Sal, we have our own ways of dealing with problems. You and your family are going to learn that." He says nothing and stares straight ahead. He's not happy, but for the moment, he keeps his opinions to himself. I start the car and head for the old mill. I'll find out what this fucker knows, and I hope Emily is still alive.

When I climb out of the car, all the brothers who were in town are here. I see Fith with Rebel on one side of him and Bear on the other. He nods at me, but I give him nothing as I stare back. This is his fault, and he'll answer for it.

I walk to the other car Guido has gotten out of, grab him by the arm, and walk him toward the old barn.

We don't use this place very often. It's a place to come and work out sensitive issues without the prying eyes of the town on us. There's only one road in and out, which the prospects will guard, making sure we know who's coming and going. Only Savage Angels will be allowed in and out, as we don't need any witnesses to what we're about to do. The brothers who are going to be in the barn are trusted and will not betray the club or me.

Pushing Guido through the barn doors, he doesn't notice the plastic covering the floor and stumbles, but doesn't fall. There's a reason we've covered a large section of the floor in the middle of the room with it. When his soldier is brought through the doors, I pull out Guido's gun and shoot him in the head. The noise is deafening, and the acrid smell of gunfire fills my nostrils. I watch as the body twitches on the floor and blood flows onto the plastic. The entire room goes quiet.

I look at Guido, shock and surprise cover his features. "This is how we handle things. I'll find who has my sister, and she'll be returned to me or this..." I motion toward his dead soldier, "... will be your fate as well." I walk toward a chair which has been placed for me at the edge of the plastic.

He stands and stares at his dead friend and asks, "This is who you do business with? These savages? There's a way to do business, and this isn't it!" he rages at Salvatore.

"You brought this on yourself. Tell him where Johnnie has the girl, and you may yet live." Salvatore also stares at the dead body on the floor, seemingly unable to look away.

"Again, with the fucking girl! Who gives a fuck about the fucking girl?" Guido yells back at him.

In two strides, Salvatore grabs him and walks him backward until he connects with a pole in the building. "*Yes*! It's about the fucking girl, Guido! She's an innocent in all of this! She has nothing to fucking do with fucking anything! How can you be so stupid?" He shoves him again and walks away.

"So, you want the girl?" Salvatore turns slowly around. "Yes, you want the girl. I could ring Johnnie and tell him to bring her to you. If, of course, you let us go, and you answer personally to Vinnie's death." Guido lays out his terms.

I watch Sal stare at Guido, not showing any emotion. I'm about to intervene when he says, "Agreed. You give us the girl, and I'll answer personally to Vinnie's death."

Guido smiles as though he has won, and then he stares at me. "Do you agree?"

I stare at Sal, who gives me the barest of nods. "Agreed." A rumble goes around the room, and I look at my men, my eyes landing on Fith. "Give him his phone. We'll abide by this ruling."

Jonas walks up to Guido and hands him his phone. Taking it, he smiles at us all, then pushes some buttons and places it to his ear. "Yeah, Johnnie, it's me. Bring the girl to..." He looks at me questioningly.

"The compound in Tourmaline," I say.

"Their compound in Tourmaline. How long will it take you to arrive?" He pauses, listens to his soldier, and he nods. "Make sure she's comfortable and unharmed. Sal will be with me." He hangs up and smiles into the phone. Without looking at anyone in particular, he says, "Now... gentlemen..." again he laughs, "... shall we?"

There's no way I'm letting this fucker live, but I have to, at least, make him think he will. I stand and say to the room, "Let's ride!" Jonas grabs Guido and pushes him toward the car. I walk over to some of my men and tilt my head toward the body. They know what to do. It isn't the first time someone has died out here. I turn and approach Sal as his phone rings.

"Yes?" he says. Then a smile plays at his lips, and he asks, "Can you stall him? How long will it take?" He pauses, listening to the call. "Good. Four hours, no more, yes?" He listens some more and says, "See you then." Looking up at me, he grins.

"Glad one of us has something to fucking smile about," I say.

"All will be revealed, my friend, all will be revealed." He does a two-fingered wave and heads out of the barn doors.

Fith approaches me and says, "Prez, I'm sorry they got Emily. If you let me, I'll make this right."

I stare at him, shake my head, and stride for the

exit. When I reach it, I say to Bear, "Bring him back to the compound."

CHAPTER 33

JOHNNIE

I hang up the phone and stare at it. We aren't supposed to be out here. We don't have permission from the Don. I can't go to any of the usual fixers as we have gone against the family, and Salvatore Agostino is well liked within it. Guido mentioned Sal, perhaps his men could help? It would be tricky, and we'd have to play them right, but if we can get away with it, we'll live.

I dial Tony, Sal's number one. "Yes?" he says

"Hey, Tony, it's Johnnie."

"Hey, Johnnie! How goes it?" he says jovially into the phone. Good, he has no idea what's going on. "There's a problem in Tourmaline. I don't know all the details, but I know those bikers have Guido and Sal. I need your help to get them back," I say, sounding desperate.

"Fuck!" He roars into the phone. "What do you need?"

"I need manpower. Can you help?"

"Abso-fucking-lutely! I can be there with five of my best in say... five hours. Where do you want to meet?" he says.

"There's a cabin on the outskirts of town. I'll send you the coordinates. See you when you arrive, Tony."

"Should I notify the family?" says Tony.

"No! No! Don't do that. It's very sensitive. It must be kept within our houses. We do not want to look weak to the Don. It would hurt all of our businesses."

"You're right, we don't want to appear weak." There's an edge to his voice. "Send me the coordinates, and we'll back you."

"Good." I hang up and send him the information. They don't need to know about the girl, and she's not at the cabin, so it makes sense to me to have them meet me there. I need to get Guido back. If we can somehow kill Sal, then we'll have his men as witnesses to the Savage Angels' betrayal.

CHAPTER 34

TONY

That fucker Johnnie thinks I can be easily manipulated. I knew the family wouldn't have done this. No way do you send a Captain out to do an underling's job, and if you do, you send him with his men to show power, strength, and to stir fear.

I phone Sal. "Yes?" he says.

"Got a call from Johnnie. He's sent me the coordinates for a cabin in the woods. Wanna bet it's where the girl is? I've told him we're five hours away, but we got a private jet, and now we're in a chopper."

"Can you stall him? How long will it take?" says Sal.

"Boss, we'll be there in three. Got your most trusted with me. I can stall him as long as you like,"

I say.

"Good. Three hours, no more, yes?" Sal sounds pleased.

"Hopefully, he won't be at the cabin. We'll do recon and let you know. You be safe, Sal. See you soon."

"See you then."

He clicks off, and I stare at the group of men surrounding me. They're all loyal to Salvatore Agostino. He's not like the other Captains. He doesn't pick his men based on which family they belong to. He picks them on their level of trust and respect. The family is supposed to be loyal to you, but I've been around long enough to watch them smile at you while they stick a knife in your back. Sal isn't like that. He intervened and saved each of us from life-threatening issues within the family. With me, he vouched for me and saved me from being blamed for a major fuck-up. I've been his number one ever since that day. He wasn't even a Captain then. You knew when he walked into a room, he commanded respect, and the older family members were wise to recognize it.

The men on the chopper are all armed, and we each have a bag full of weapons. All eyes are on me.

"Guido Lamberti is trying to gain control of our business. He's trying to blame Sal for the gun-running issue. The family doesn't know, but Guido is the enforcer for the family, so we have to be careful. We must tell no one, we can't have it blow back on Salvatore or us. Are we clear?" They all nod.

Lorenzo looks at me and asks, "The family doesn't know?" Then he smiles. "I've never liked Guido. Can we kill him?"

"Yes, and whoever is with him, but we can tell no one. I've asked around, and they have not told anyone they're here. They set up Sal to kill him or blame him, either way, they wanted him dead."

He nods at me. "That fucker set me up. If it weren't for Sal, I'd be dead. So, what's the plan?" Lorenzo has worked for Sal for two years. He's loyal, six foot three, and full of muscle and determination, but doesn't always think things through.

"Johnnie has sent me the coordinates for a cabin. He's probably got the girl there. He's had her for hours, so she'll be in a bad way... we all know what he's like," I say with a sneer. It's no secret Johnnie is a rapist. Sal doesn't tolerate the abuse of women. We who follow him are the same. "Sal likes this woman. Her name is Emily, and she's the sister of the leader of the Savage Angels." Some shake their heads and stare at the floor, and Lorenzo raises his eyebrows. "We're to find her, kill Johnnie, dispose of him, then make sure the girl receives medical attention."

"Will Sal still want her after Johnnie has finished with her?" says Marco.

I shrug. "Have you ever heard him say he liked a woman? But you're right, I don't know."

"I've only ever seen him with party girls. In all the time I've known him, I have never seen him with a woman more than once and never heard him say he likes one of them," says Lorenzo.

"Guido is a dead motherfucker for that. He'd have put Johnnie up to it. Looking forward to killing the fucker," says Stefano.

I nod at them. The rest of the trip is done in silence as we all contemplate what we're about to do. If we kill Guido, it leaves a massive hole in the family. I'm not sure Salvatore wants that position. Sal is a force to be reckoned with, but he has lines he won't cross. There are others who could fill the void, but first, we have to make Guido disappear and then sit back and watch the aftermath.

Hopefully, Don Abruzzi will not suspect us, and he'll give Sal more territory.

CHAPTER 35

EMILY

I have a fire going, and I'm cold. It's night, and I can hear animals roaming about, calling to each other.

At first light, I'm going to backtrack and hope he's not still there. I am scared. It hasn't even been a full day, but I'm thirsty. I need clothes. I know I'm being overly dramatic and I am not even sure which direction I ran in, but hopefully, I can follow my own tracks. I won't survive another day.

I wish I could go back to Salvatore and try to explain how I feel about guns. There was definitely a connection with him. I've never had a man buy me so many things, and he has no idea what it meant to me. I wish I could talk to Dane and ask him why he abandoned me, and I hope I can bury my father along with all the baggage he left me with.

I sharpen my stake on a rock as I let my thoughts wander. If the man is still there, I'll kill him. No one will ever violate me like that again. When I think about what he said he was going to do, I shudder. Although my hands are sore, they're doing what I need them to do, and the piece of wood has a sharper point on it now. I'll never be so vulnerable again.

I hope someone is looking for me. I hope I matter to someone.

My feet are cut, and with each step I take, excruciating pain shoots through me. I'm trying to hold onto the stake, but my hands are awfully sore. When I woke up, they were all cramped. I've flexed them out, but I really hope no one is at the cabin—if I can find it.

It's barely daylight, and I slowly follow my tracks. It takes me about two hours to get there. I can see a group of men going in and out, they're all dressed in black, and all have guns. One of them holds up my dress to the others, and they all stare at it, then one of them says something and shakes his head.

I hear a rumbling noise, and then the area in front of the cabin is full of motorbikes. The man with my dress walks up to Dane and hands it to him. He stands there shaking his head, then I see Salvatore, and I hear him yell, "Have you found her body? Was there evidence she's dead? Blood?"

Without exposing myself to the entire population of Tourmaline, I have no idea how to get someone's attention. I am naked in the woods, crouching behind a bush.

The sound of breaking branches startles me, and I stand up and turn around. It's Jonas, and he has his hands up as he says, "It's okay, Em, put your weapon down, baby. You're safe."

My hand managed to grip my stake, after all. He slowly walks toward me, taking his jacket off. He never breaks eye contact. I hadn't realized how nice his eyes were—pale green and full of concern. He's about three feet from me and holds out his jacket. I snatch it and put it on. It barely covers my ass, but at least I have a level of modesty back. With a mutual understanding, he whistles—loud. A silence fills the air, and he points to the men behind me. I grip his jacket around me and turn without letting go of my stake.

Salvatore strides toward me, and I back up right into Jonas. He slows his pace with hands up like Jonas did. "Amare, you're safe. I'll not hurt you."

All I do is stare at him. My throat is sore, and I

can feel tears run down my cheeks. He slowly approaches and holds out his hand. I stare at it for a moment, then drop my stake and launch myself into his arms, crying uncontrollably.

I feel him lift me, and all the while, he whispers to me, "Va tutto bene, amore, sei protetto, lo sei." *<It's all right, love, you are protected, you are safe.>* Over and over, he repeats these words to me, soothing me to my core. I feel safe in his arms.

I am safe.

As he carries me toward a car, I see Dane striding toward us. When he reaches us, he says, "I'll drive, you hold her tight." His eyes flick to mine, and I'm surprised at the level of compassion I find there. "You're safe, Em. No one will hurt you ever again." His mouth goes into a hard line. Then he whistles loudly and raises his hand, signaling for his men to leave.

Sal places me on the back seat of a car, then goes around to the other side, climbs in, and drags me across, so I sit on his lap with his arms around me.

Dane climbs into the driver's seat. "Emily, I'm so sorry this happened to you. I'm going to take you to Doc Jordan's, okay?"

I nod at him but don't make eye contact. Salvatore's arms tighten around me, and I look him in the eyes. "Do you have any water?" I croak out.

He looks to Dane, who yells out the window, "Does anyone have water?"

Jonas walks up to Salvatore's window and passes me a bottle of water. "Here you go, Em. I'll be seeing you soon." Then he smiles at me, and his entire face seems to light up. My hands can barely hold the bottle as I smile at him and nod. "Savage Angels' colors look good on you." He smiles again but shifts his gaze to Salvatore, who presses the button to wind up the window.

"Let's take her to your doctor, yes?" Sal says to Dane forcefully.

Dane chuckles. "I'm on it."

Salvatore touches my hand, and I wince. My other hand grips the bottle while I try to open it, but I can't grip the lid properly. He takes it from me and undoes it. The water feels fantastic as it slides down my throat. I smile at Sal and wriggle off his lap and sit beside him with his arm around me. I then reposition myself with my back against the car door and my legs over his lap. His hands lightly touch my legs. There are cuts and scrapes over both of them, including the slice on my right leg from the cabin window when I escaped. My left foot has a deep gash on the arch, and I have stubbed toes on both my feet. My hair is down and matted, and then there are my hands. I feel like I am bruised everywhere.

I'm staring at my hands when Sal reaches over and lifts my chin. "You know you're safe, and nothing like that will ever happen to you again, yes?"

I nod at him and drink more water, not paying attention to my surroundings. When the car stops, I look up, and we're outside Doc Jordan's. My eyes go to Sal.

"I can't walk, would you mind helping me?" My voice waivers, and I watch Sal wince.

"Anything for you, amare. Can you slide over to this side, and I'll carry you from there?" His voice is full of concern. I nod at him. Opening the door, he climbs out. I look around, and there are people everywhere. I hear the rumble of the Savage Angels as they go past, back to their compound. I shuffle to the edge of the seat. Sal puts one arm under my legs and the other around my back, then carries me into Doc Jordan's.

The waiting room is full, but the receptionist takes one look at me and ushers all three of us into a room.

Sal puts me up on a bed, and I immediately lay down. The frazzled, rude receptionist from my previous visit now has nothing but concern on her face.

"Gentlemen, you'll have to wait outside. Now." She's firm with them and opens the door.

"Emily, we'll be outside," says Dane. Salvatore nods.

When she shuts the door, she approaches me. "Honey, let's put a gown on you." She opens a drawer and pulls out a gown. She hands it to me, then pulls a curtain across. Taking the jacket off, I slip on the gown, but it ties up at the back, and I can't do it.

"Could you... umm... help me?" I ask, and my voice cracks.

She opens the curtain and goes behind me to do up the gown. "Honey, I'll go get Doc now, okay?" I nod and smile at her as she leaves the room.

The gown is blue and reaches down to my knees. I'm playing with the hem as the doctor comes into the room.

I look up at him, and he smiles, then I watch it slowly fall off his face. His step falters. I smile at him. "Hey, Doc, sorry I look such a mess. Who knew Tourmaline could be so..." A tear escapes from my eye and rolls down my cheek.

"Okay, Emily, let's take a look at you."

"Doc, do you have somewhere I could shower before you examine me? I really need to wash myself off," I say, avoiding all eye contact.

"Emily, do we need to take swabs before you shower? Is there anything you'd like to tell me?" He's bent over, staring into my eyes.

I shake my head. "He didn't have a chance to, not really." I stare at the floor, my face burning.

"Not really? Sweetheart, if he... penetrated you, there will be DNA, and we need to collect it."

"He didn't have a chance to... insert himself." I'm mortified. I don't want to talk about this with the doctor or anyone.

"Okay then, Emily, let's put you into a shower. Is it all right if Maggie helps you?"

I nod at him, and he leaves the room. A short time later, Maggie comes in with a wheelchair. "Jump in, honey, let's get you cleaned up." She smiles at me as I sit in the wheelchair.

She opens the door and pushes me out. Dane and Salvatore stand side by side. I smile at them both and say, "Going for a shower, won't be long." I'm sure my smile looks more like a grimace.

Once we're in the bathroom, Maggie looks at me. "Sixty-eight percent of all rapes are never reported to the police. Ninety-eight percent of rapists will never spend a day in jail. Honey, if you have been attacked, you need to say something."

I look up at her, and her eyes are full of empathy. "I don't know." I breakdown. She wraps me in her arms and strokes my hair. "I don't know."

"Honey, I'll be with you, but we need Doc Jordan to check you out. If someone did something, they may have a sexually transmitted disease, which they might have given you, and, honey, you could be hurt." Maggie continues to hold me and stroke my hair for what feels like forever.

"All right, Maggie, please wheel me back. If you stay with me, I'll let Doc Jordan examine me."

She stands up, grabs some tissues, and wipes my face. "Let's do this," she says with a small smile. She opens the door and wheels me back to the other room. Both Dane and Sal raise their eyebrows.

"Is everything okay?" asks Dane, sounding concerned.

I make eye contact with him. "Yes, we need Doc to check something out first." I try to smile, but I know it probably looks forced.

Sal opens the door to the room, then drops to his knees in front of me. "Whatever Doc finds and whatever you need to do, I need you to know if you want to talk, I'm here. No matter what you say or tell me, I'll think no less of you. Do you understand me, amare?" I look at him, and a few strands of hair have fallen over his eye. I reach out, push them off his face, and nod as a tear rolls down my cheek. He wipes it away and gives me a smile full of sympathy. No matter what he says, he'll never look at me the same way again. He stands and kisses my forehead, then moves out of the way as Maggie wheels me into the room.

I'm on the bed, and Maggie is holding my hand when Doc Jordan comes in and says, "Okay, Emily, before we do anything, can you tell me what happened?"

"I woke up on a table, naked. There was a man. He put his hands on me... everywhere, and he said he'd been playing with me for a while," I whisper, and I realize I'm squeezing Maggie's hand really tight. I loosen my grip, and when I look at her, she has tears in her eyes.

"Good girl, honey, you did really well." She puts both of her hands around mine.

"Emily, I need to examine you. Now, it won't take long, but it's not going to be pleasant for you. If you need me to stop, please say so, okay?"

I nod and close my eyes tight. Taking a deep breath, I try to imagine I'm anywhere but on this bed.

Doc was right, the examination wasn't pleasant. There was minimal trauma and no fluids on or in me.

Doc stands next to me as he says, "I don't believe he got to insert... I mean, it doesn't appear that he—"

"Are you saying I wasn't raped?" I whisper.

"No, Emily. I'm saying it appears he only used his hands, but it doesn't mean you weren't raped."

I understand what it means, the bastard still violated me. "Thank you. Can I please go shower now?"

He rubs my arms. "Of course."

Maggie wheels me back into the hallway. I don't

make eye contact with anyone, and neither Dane nor Salvatore attempt to approach me. Once inside the bathroom, Maggie turns on the shower and wheels me to it.

"Now, honey, take as long as you like. Try to give those legs of yours a good wash. It's okay if the wheelchair gets wet. Would you like me to wheel you closer to the shower?"

"Yes, please, my feet hurt." I pause and ask, "Maggie, could you help me? Please?"

"Yes, honey, it's what I'm here for, so let's get you cleaned up."

CHAPTER 36

SALVATORE

I watch as she's wheeled past me, not making eye contact with either of us. I turn and stare at Doc Jordan, who's collecting his swabs and God knows what else.

I walk into the room. "Was she raped? Did he rape her?" My tone is gruff, and I'm to the point.

Doc rubs his hand over his face. "It's up to Emily to disclose that. I'm bound by law not to discuss it. I will tell you I need the sheriff to talk to her."

He has told me without telling me. By law, he has to report this to the police. I nod, and I turn to look at Dane. I shake my head in the negative at him.

He walks up to the Doctor. "I know this isn't something I should ask you, Doc, but we know who's done this, and we'll... deal with him in-house.

Is there any way you could make this go away?"

Doc Jordan stands and stares at each of us. He sighs and says, "I can get into a lot of trouble. I can lose my license."

"No one but us will know. We wouldn't betray you." Dane nods in agreement.

"If Emily doesn't want to follow this through, I'd be okay with it," says Doc.

"What about the nurse?" I ask.

"She'll do whatever Emily wants her to do. It's no secret, but years ago, Maggie was gang- raped in New York. She is and always will be on the victim's... survivor's side."

I nod at Doc and walk outside. I can hear Dane talking to him, but I block it out. I can feel my rage go from explosive to white-hot, simmering under the surface. I haven't felt this way since my father. Walking to the bathroom door where Emily is, I'm staring at it, trying to decide the best course of action, when Doc puts his hand on my shoulder.

"You'll need to give her time. I'll let her tell you, but it's not as bad as it could've been." I look into Doc's eyes, and he looks down. He shakes his head and goes back into the examination room, leaving me to stand in front of the door. Alone.

From the moment I met Emily, she has attracted trouble. There's a vulnerability about her, but when we found her in the woods, she wasn't broken. She was armed and ready. Even in the car, she positioned herself facing me. Perhaps she'll find an inner strength, one she didn't know she had. The door opens, and Maggie is standing there. When she moves, I can see Emily, clean from the trauma of the past twenty-four hours.

Unfortunately, the wounds, both physical and emotional, will not be overcome so quickly.

"How are you?" I ask, desperately wanting to hold her.

"Better, I feel so much better." She lifts her foot, which is now clean, and you can see she'll probably need stitches. "But this, hurts. Maggie used some antibacterial wash on it and aggravated it, so now it hurts bad."

I chuckle at her. "Hurts bad?"

"Yeah, hurts bad." Then she smiles at me.

"Well, I'd best move out of the way so Doc can help you to... feel good."

"Thank you, Salvatore. Will you wait for me?"

"Amare, I'd wait for you even if you didn't want me to." Then I move out of her way and watch as she's wheeled back to the doctor. Dane smiles at her, and she gives him a slight nod.

I walk back to him. "Doc is on board. My question to you is... what do you want to do with Guido and Johnnie?"

I'm surprised he'd ask. This is, after all, his town, his rules. "They can't be allowed to live. I am certain he didn't have permission to go after me, but there's also the problem with a member of your MC undercutting us. What are you going to do about it?"

He rubs both hands over his face. He's taller than me and built. His black wife-beater strains at the arms as he does this.

"This is a major fuck-up for me. Every which way I look at it, I look weak." He looks me in the eyes. "I'm trying to pull the club out of illegal activities." I raise my eyebrows at him, and he continues, "We have a garage in almost every chapter, we have strip clubs all over and in some states, brothels. We treat the girls well. No one is forced into anything. We also have high-class escorts in some of the major cities. Most of the chapters steer clear of narcotics, but it's easy money. Just like running guns."

"You said you were unaware of that," I say, keeping eye contact.

"Yeah, man, I was. I let a little old lady, who I thought was my friend, trick us into guarding her shipments, and then one of my men kept it going and expanded it. All without my fucking knowledge. I'm fucked every way you look at it."

"No, if you find out how your man managed to do it, pay tribute to Don Abruzzi and kill your man to keep him quiet. No one needs to know."

"My MC doesn't run that way. Some of the boys already know about Fith. He'll be dealt with, but so will I."

"You could still keep this under wraps, and you know it. Don't sacrifice yourself for some misplaced loyalty. Look at me. Guido Lamberti is the enforcer for the Abruzzi family. I have been in and around this family my whole life, and he was going to kill me. For what? More territory? Real estate is where I make most of my money and playing the stock market. Not guns, not drugs, and certainly not whores. The old ways are dying, and if you don't move with the times, you'll lose everything."

"My loyalty to my MC isn't misplaced. I'll let them judge me, and I will live with the outcome. But I'll not give up my presidency easily," says Dane with a snarl.

The door to the examination room opens, and Emily sits in a wheelchair with a blue gown on and the Savage Angels cut over it. I have to admit, she looks good.

"Can you walk, Em, or do we need to hire you a wheelchair?" asks Dane.

"She's to stay off her foot for a couple of days. You can keep the chair. I'll give you some crutches, too. But she'll need someone to take care of her for at least a week," says the Doc, staring straight at me.

"I'll make the necessary arrangements," I say.

"No," says Emily.

We all stare at her, and she smiles. I feel my chest constrict. My hand goes to my heart. "You need help, amare, please let me."

"Yes, you can help, but..." and she moves her gaze to Dane, "... I know you have holiday rentals. I've looked at your website, and they're fully self-contained. If I could rent one of those, if you have any available, I'd appreciate it."

I'm surprised by her self-assurance. I expected her to be a little needier. I look at Dane, and I can see him having an internal battle.

He eventually says, "You can have one of the cottages, but it will be free of charge. I don't have anyone staying out at the house at the moment either, so you're welcome to stay at my home. This is my preference."

Emily shakes her head. "No, I don't know you well enough to stay in your home. And I can't stay in one of your cottages for free. It wouldn't be right."

"How about I agree to charge you a nominal fee? Please don't argue with me, Em. I even have one that's wheelchair compatible. It's nice." He flicks his gaze to me. "Sal, you'll take care of her? I have room in my house."

His tone and meaning are clear. Interesting, he doesn't want his sister to share a room with me. I smile at him and am about to answer when Emily beats me to it.

"Thank you so much for letting Salvatore stay in your home. That's perfect."

I smile at them both and nod. "I need to retrieve my car from the motel, and I need to do some shopping, too."

"Shopping?" asks Dane.

"Yes, my friend, shopping. I only have the clothes on my back. Can I leave Emily in your capable hands while I attend to business?" Dane knows I have other issues to attend to—Guido and Johnnie. He nods at me, and I bend, kiss Emily on the forehead, as I leave, she grabs my arm.

"You'll be back before dark?" she asks, and I'm surprised to see fear in her eyes.

"Yes, amare, I'll be an hour at most."

She nods and takes a deep breath, the fear appears to seep away. "An hour? Good. Do you know where it is?"

"No, but Dane will send it to me." I kiss her forehead again and smile at her. I nod at the doctor and give Dane a two-fingered wave as I head for the front of the medical practice.

As I hit the sidewalk, a hand lands on my shoulder, turning it's Dane. I quirk an eyebrow at him, and he lets his hand fall.

"My home is on the outskirts of town. If you follow Main Street that way..." he points, "... and keep going you'll come to an intersection. Turn left and keep going up. I'll text you the exact address."

"Thank you."

He's a big man, and it's interesting watching him

shuffle from foot to foot. Clearly, he has something on his mind. Dane stops moving and levels me with his stare.

"My sister—"

"Is someone I intend to get to know."

He frowns at me. "I get that." Dane sucks in a breath. "You need to understand that *I* want to get to know her, too. She's the only family I have, and our relationship is fractured. I only ask you don't get in the way of that."

His honesty takes me by surprise.

I dip my head. "Family is important. I have no intention of undermining your relationship with Emily."

Dane stands straighter and lifts his chin. "Good."

He turns and walks back inside, leaving me to my thoughts. I need clothes, and to talk to Tony. My men arrived and captured Johnnie with no kind of altercation, which is strange. He has to know we're going to kill him, or perhaps he believes he's too high up in the family to be touched. Normally, he'd be correct, but the family doesn't know we're here. Don Abruzzi has not phoned me back, so I don't have to apprise him of the situation here in Tourmaline. It does not sit well with me, but Guido has left me no choice.

I've purchased new clothes and am making my way back to the motel. I can see Tony as he talks to Adelynn. He smiles at her, and I bet he's using all his best lines. She's a fine-looking woman, but from the little I've spoken to her, I know he doesn't have a chance in hell.

When I get closer, I do a chin lift, and he waves. Adelynn turns, and she smiles. Maybe I'm wrong, maybe he does have a chance in hell.

"Adelynn, Tony, how are things?" I ask, trying to sound casual. I need to sit down with my men and run over all of our options—idle conversation isn't something I want to do.

"Mr. Agostino, you're good for business! Thank you for recommending your friends stay here." She looks genuinely happy. It's not tourist season, so I'm guessing business must be slow.

"My pleasure, Adelynn, and please call me Salvatore. I hope Tony has been behaving himself."

She giggles. "He's been a complete gentleman! Now, I need to go back to work, but if you need anything, you all know where I am." Her smile is huge as she walks away, and we both watch her.

I look at Tony and watch the smile fade from his

face. "She was asking about Emily. Told her she went hiking and got lost, and we found her. It's a small town, boss. Someone might talk."

"Agreed." I walk toward my room. "Fuck, Tony, you ever been in this much fucking shit? You ever had a boss come after you like this? What the fuck did I ever do to Guido, anyway?" I open the door, and I step in, with Tony following me.

"It's a shitstorm, all right. Boss, the boys want to have a round table with you on this. I told them this is your show, and we'll do as you say, but I also said I'd let you know what they wanted."

A round-table meeting. It's been a while since we've done that. I started it when we took Lorenzo on board. He was a loose cannon who could've betrayed us and what I was trying to build—he saw the light, though, and everyone knows I take care of my men. Basically, we all sit down. I let them voice their concerns, and we talk through all of their objections and comments, but I still have the last say. It's good for me too—sometimes it's hard to see all the angles.

"Yes, I was going to suggest it. I even know where we can have it. The Savage Angels have a room at their compound where they have their sit-downs, their Church as they call it."

"You want me to clear it with one of them first?" says Tony.

"No, I'll do it since I've got Reynolds' number, but

first, I'm having a shower. I need to change into some clean clothes. Take the boys to Bettie's Café for some good food. Be nice to the waitress. Her name's Rosie, and she's a good girl. Feed her the story about Emily getting lost while hiking and how we found her. It'll be around town in a heartbeat." He nods at me. "And, Tony, watch the local sheriff. He's from our part of the country, and he has a serious hard-on for Guido. Play dumb if you run into him and don't piss him off. Are we clear?"

"Boss, come on, I'm a nice guy!" he says, arms spread wide and a big grin on his face. "I'll have this entire town eating out of my hand!"

"The sheriff is a hard-ass. You've been warned," I say over my shoulder as I walk into the bathroom.

CHAPTER 37

TRUTH

I have no idea how Kat can stand to live out here in the middle of fucking nowhere. It's a nice town—pretty, even—but no clubs, only a couple of bars, both of which belong to her boyfriend. The limousine pulls up in front of Kat's house. I'm surprised. I thought we were going to Dane's house. Dave winds down his window and puts in the code to open the gate. It's not working, and he punches the keys harder.

"Dave, man, does it occur to you she's changed the code?" I ask.

"No, she gave me the new one!"

I climb out of the car, walk to the intercom, and push the button. "Yo! My wild, wilderness-loving rocker! Open the fucking gate before Dave breaks the keypad!" I say with fake enthusiasm.

Her front door flies open, and she runs across the lawn toward us. That's our girl, always running full-on into anything. I can see some of her Savage Angels behind her, and they don't look happy.

"Truth! Baby! So good to see you!" she yells.

"Well, let us the fuck in, then!" I say with a grin.

Kat walks to the gate and punches in the codes. The main gate slowly opens, but she opens the side gate to let me in. I take two steps, and Kat launches herself into my embrace. This woman gives the best hugs. I think it's because of her height. She just fits into your body so well.

"My retired rocker, how are you?"

"Fuck that, you know I'm well, and you know I'm happy, but why is Dave babysitting you?" She pulls back and looks up at me. "What's wrong, Truth? Are you okay?"

That's my girl, straight to the point. "Well, my... Kat, I'm fine."

"Wow! You suck at lying! Fine, I'll leave you alone for now, but I'll find out." She pushes out of my embrace. "Come on, let's go get Dave, and you can see the modifications I've made to my home!" She looks happy as she drags me toward her front door.

"Katarina Saunders! Where's my hello?" asks Dave with a small amount of impatience.

She laughs and runs to him. Her level of energy

never ceases to amaze me. As she hugs Dave, I take her in. Her hair is longer. In fact, I think it's the longest I've ever seen it on her—it's past her ass and has blonde highlights. She also has a tan and radiates happiness. She's one of those women who gets better looking the older she gets—mind you, she's only twenty-eight. I'm pushing thirty, and my family life has gone to hell, so I feel ninety.

"Come on." Kat grabs us both by the arms. "Come see what I've done! You'll love the studio, Truth! I built you a little podium so you can sing from it, and I got you a present!" she shrieks the last word. Kat is the only woman I know who more than loves presents. I mean, you can give her a fucking chocolate bar, and so long as you say it's a present, she'll be stoked. She also loves giving presents—they're always over the top and too much, but she never cares. You can tell she wants you to be happy because she normally tries extremely hard to find you what you absolutely want. She's more than generous, and over the years, I have discovered it's one way for her to show you she loves you.

Dave is, of course, simply happy to be in her presence. He has always thought of her as his daughter. Even when I first joined the band, he made it clear I was to stay away from his princess. It's funny, I never really looked at her that way. Don't get me wrong, she's five foot four of hotness, but I felt it in my bones it would wreck our relationship. It's nice to have a little bit of sexual tension. I know she'd never go there, but it's fun to try.

We're dragged into what was her living room. It's been completely remodeled into a studio. The booth where we perform is amazing.

"I had to replace the glass on one wall, but apart from that, this room was really easy to convert," says Kat.

"How come you didn't cover it up?" I ask.

"What, and lose the view? Are you crazy?" She laughs.

"I see your point, now... where's my present?"

Dave raises his eyebrows at me as she runs away to find it. When she leaves the room, he says, "You okay?"

"Yeah, man. You didn't need to bring me. I'm fine, really!"

"No, you're not," Dave says in a firm tone. "She'll be good for you. She brings out your good side."

I nod. It's true. She has a way about her, which makes me shine. I can't deny it. "Yeah, she does."

"She does what?" Kat bounds back into the room, holding a guitar. She thrusts it at me, and I take it.

"Kat, is this what I think it is?" I ask as I smile at her.

"Yep! Wasn't easy to find, and I had to do a lot of begging, but I knew how much you wanted it, so I got it for you," she says as she bounces up and down on her feet.

She's managed to get me my hero's guitar. When I started playing in my hometown, there was an old guy who taught me everything. His name was Samuel Goldsmith, and he was a mentor to me, and he played gigs around my hometown. He never made it big—never wanted to—but his guitar-playing was sublime. When he died, I was promised his guitar, but he didn't put it in his will, and his family said they would sell it to me but wouldn't give it to me. By then, I had made it big with The Grinders, so they asked for a million dollars. I could've paid, but it was the principle— they knew he wanted me to have it. I said I wouldn't pay, and then a year later, I contacted them, and they said they sold it in a garage sale. I was devastated. I should've paid for it in the first place. Kat went through it all with me, so she knew how much I wanted it.

"But how? It disappeared. How the fuck did you track it down?" I ask with disbelief.

"Oh, honey, they knew who bought it. They were mad at losing their million dollars. Fuckers. The youngest son, Dylan, told me who had it. The man was Samuel's friend, and he owned a bar Samuel played at. He didn't want to sell, but when I told him it was for you, he gave it to me. But it comes with strings."

"What kind of strings?" I ask, and Dave chuckles.

"I promised we'd play at his bar one night. I told him he couldn't advertise it, said we'd all drop in and jam for a night. And I promised him you'd play this guitar in honor of Samuel."

"You got a good deal." Emotion floods my voice.

She tries to hug me while I hold the guitar. "Oh, honey, I'd do anything for you, you know that, right?"

I smirk at her. "Anything, my teasing temptress?"

Dave steps in. "That's enough of that. Now, princess, I'm tired. Are we staying here?"

She holds my gaze. "No, we're staying at Dane's." Then she grabs Dave's hand. "But before we go, you haven't said what you think of the studio. I think it's great, and I've been helping Dan Kelly to produce his album. He's staying here at the moment. He fired his management team, and they stupidly released him. Dave, he's going to be huge, but don't tell him I told you, his ego is big enough!"

I watch as Dave's eyes twinkle at the thought of new blood. His smile grows bigger as he says, "Your studio, my princess, looks good, but as we all know, it can look good, but if it can't hold a tune, it won't last."

"Are we talking about my studio now or something else?" asks Kat.

He chuckles and kisses her forehead. "You have done an amazing job. I'm impressed, especially with the equipment, and I bet it cost you a pretty penny, no doubt." He puts his arm around her waist. "Now, take me to Dan Kelly."

I'm left with Samuel's guitar, so I walk into the booth and plug it in. I don't realize I have an audience as I play "Heaven." I have my eyes closed, lost in my thoughts of Samuel and what he meant to me. The guitar isn't a particularly good one, but I can play "Heaven" in my sleep. I'm thankful to Kat for retrieving a childhood memento. Samuel would be pleased. As I come to the end of "Heaven," applause fills the room. I look up and see two women standing there with three of the Savage Angels.

I grin up at them. "What would you like to hear?"

One of the Savage Angels asks for "Enter Sandman" by Metallica.

"Does anyone play drums? It'll sound better with drums?"

One of the women comes into the booth. She must be five foot eleven, wearing a pair of those denim shorts which leave nothing to the imagination and a singlet. Her hair is shaved off, and she has a tattoo near her left eye. It looks like a music note.

She smiles at me and says, "I play a little. It'll be an honor to play with you, Truth."

I smile at her. A fan, and a good-looking fan at that. Today just got better. "Well, let's see how you play."

I start, then she comes in with the drums, and damn, she's good. She sits with her legs apart, and she's not wearing any panties. My cock is hard. I can't take my eyes away from her pussy. I have my back to our small audience, so they can't see what has me hypnotized. When we get to the end of the song, she licks her lips, and my cock strains against my jeans. I'm thankful I have the guitar in front of me.

Our audience claps, and as I turn around, she comes up beside me, grabs my hand, and holds it over our heads, and yells, "Woo-hoo! I played with Truth from The Grinders!" Oh, she's played with me all right, and I intend to play with her. It's been a while since I've fucked someone.

"Well, my delicious drummer, you can play!" I say with a smirk.

"Oh, Truth, you have no idea."

I hope to God I'm reading her correctly. Kat and Dave, and I assume, Dan Kelly, clap as well. I do a bow, and so does my drummer.

"So, I see the guitar works well!" says Kat as she stares at my drummer.

I drawl at her. "You have no idea." A smile creeps across my face.

"Truth, your drummer is Amy, and this is Sandy." She points at Dan and says, "Sandy is Dan's sister, and Amy plays drums in Dan's band. We're thinking of calling them Dark Ink. And you know the brothers, don't you?" asks Kat.

"Yeah, we've met before." I give them a chin lift. Sandy's cute. A little bit mousy for my taste. She has dark hair worn up in a ponytail, and she's curvy. She's obviously nervous, as she can barely look at me. Dan puts his arm around her and gives me a look, and I smile. It's nice her big brother is protective. I look at Amy.

"So, where are you staying?"

Before she can answer, Dan says, "She's staying here with me and Sandy."

I can tell from his tone and posture he's trying to look out for his girls, but Amy is mine. I nod at him and look back at Amy. "You want to come to Dane's house and have a look around?" I smirk at her.

She moves her head up and down so quickly, it looks like a bobble doll. Yeah, I'm reading her correctly—she's up for some fun!

"Sounds cool. I'd like that, I would like that a lot," says Amy.

"Okay, those who are coming, come... those who are staying, stay... but let's get on the road. I'm tired," says Dave.

"Kat, can I leave my present here?" I ask.

"Sure, honey, I made a special spot for it on the wall at the back. Go look, you'll find it."

I put the guitar away and walk toward Amy, grab her hand, and say to the rest of them, "Later. Have a good one."

I rub my thumb across her knuckles and open the limousine door, and she climbs in, followed by Kat. Dave walks around the other side, and before I climb in, Dan says, "What time will you have her back?"

"Not sure, but I'll see she arrives home safely. Have a good night." I wink at him.

The trip to Dane's house isn't a long one. When we pull up in the driveway, Dane is there with a beautiful woman in a wheelchair. She has bandages on her feet and hands, and she looks like she's in a hospital gown. From the scowl on her face, she isn't happy.

We all climb out, and Kat walks to the woman in the wheelchair and crouches down to her level. "Hello, Emily, it's so nice to meet you. I'm Kat, are you okay?"

"I'm fine. Could you please take me to the cottage that's equipped to handle a wheelchair?" Her tone is cold.

"Of course, I'll—"

"No, Kat, she isn't going to one of the cottages. She's staying here in the house," says Dane with more than a little bit of irritation.

Kat stands up, squares her shoulders. "Dane Reynolds, this is your sister, and she is obviously very upset. She's injured, and she wants to go to a cottage. Now go and find the keys to it before she decides she wants to go back into town."

Dane looks up to the heavens, looks back at Kat, shakes his head, and goes inside. Kat turns back around and crouches down to Emily.

"Honey, he means well. You need to give him time. Although, looking at you, it should be the other way around. What happened to you?"

Dane walks back out onto the veranda and hands Kat the keys. "Kat, could you please take Emily to the cottage, and I'll make sure everyone else is settled?"

"Dane, my boy, I can see to myself. I'll take the same room I always have, yes? And it's good to see you. Black t-shirts really look good on you," says Dave as he makes his way into the house as if he owns it.

I wink at Dane. "Dane, do you know Amy?" He nods, and I continue, "She'll be staying with me for a while." He gives me the barest of smiles, then looks toward Kat and his sister. I have no idea what's going on, and right now, all I want to do is fuck this woman. My cock needs to be released.

"So, Amy, want to see my room?"

She smiles at me. "Lead the way."

Picking up my suitcase, I grab her hand and practically run up the stairs. When we arrive at my room, I open the door and push her inside.

She laughs. "So, I thought you were taking me on a tour of the house?" she says as she smiles smugly and walks around the room. I shut the door, put my suitcase down, and stalk toward her. She backs up against one wall and smiles at me.

I put a hand on either side of her head and push my body up against hers. "I like the ink on your face. Tell me, amorous Amy, do you have any more?"

Her breath catches. "Any more what?" she whispers.

I grin and stare at her mouth. "Any more ink? Or should I look for myself?"

She moves her head forward, so she can whisper into my ear, "How about you look for yourself?" Then she sucks on my earlobe.

I chuckle. "Let the games begin."

Moving my hands down to her breasts, I brush over both her nipples with my thumbs. She gasps. I love it when they respond to me. I kiss her neck and then suck. She tastes slightly salty, and I like it. She moans as I reach down, grab the hem of her black singlet, and pull it up over her head. I step back and look at her.

"No ink?"

She smiles. "I was going to have my head done, but chickened out and only got the music note. It's why I have a shaved head. It's normally a little longer than this."

"You wear it well. Baby, I'm covered in ink. Let's move this to the bed." I move backward. She takes a step toward me and stops. I keep going until my knees hit the bed. I look at her crotch and lick my lips. "Come here."

She reaches around and undoes her bra, letting her full breasts loose. She bends forward slightly as she undoes her shorts, and I watch her breasts sway freely as she pushes the skimpy scrap of denim over her hips, letting it drop to the floor. My cock is hard thinking about what I'm going to do to her. I stare at her, enjoying the show, but she's not moving.

"Amy, I said come here." This time I'm more forceful.

Slowly, she walks toward me and smiles. "I like to be dominated and told what to do. Can you do that?"

"On your knees and take off my boots," I say, not taking my eyes off her crotch. She hesitates, so I say aggressively, "Do it now."

She kneels in front of me and takes off my boots. Her hands are on my thighs, and my cock can't take being trapped in my jeans a moment longer.

I stand. "Undo my jeans." She struggles with my belt but eventually removes it, then she stands and doubles it over, snapping it in front of my face. "Jeans!" I say a little more loudly.

Amy undoes my jeans. I knead her breasts as she's freeing my cock. She pulls my jeans down and takes my underwear at the same time. When Amy gets to my knees, I sit down. My cock is erect, and I need to fuck her now.

"Straddle me."

She looks at me and traces the tattoos on my shoulders with her fingertips.

"You have so many tattoos, you hardly have any space left." Amy grasps my cock. I close my eyes as she strokes it up and down. "Condoms. Do you have any?"

I open my eyes and smile. "In my suitcase, front pocket." I watch her walk to my suitcase—she has a nice ass. Amy bends over, giving me a full view of her pussy. Unable to resist, I grab my cock and stroke myself.

"Stop. That's my job." She walks back to me, opens the foil wrapper, and places the condom in her mouth.

She kneels in front of me, then, with her mouth and hands, she places the condom on my cock. I lay back as she sucks and uses her tongue on the sensitive nerves near the tip. I reach down and grab her—the stubble on her head feels weird to touch, but I like it. I move her up and down, enjoying all the different sensations. I don't want to blow into her mouth, but it feels so good.

"You keep doing that, and I'm not going to last long." She stops sucking me, and I feel her lips on my stomach as she licks her way up to my nipples, both of which are pierced. I feel her tongue play with my piercings, but I'm way past slow lovemaking.

"Straddle me, now."

"Not yet."

I sit up and flip us, so I'm on top. "You said you like to be dominated. Do as you're told," I say with a growl.

"But I'm not there yet."

"Baby, from the moment you sat down at those drums, I have been hard. I'll get you there, but first I need to fuck you, and I'm going to do it hard and fast. You said you liked to be dominated, so spread your legs 'cause I'm going to fuck you."

I kneel between her legs, spread them, and push her knees up. The tip of my cock is at her lips, and I slowly push myself into her pussy. She gasps as my cock slides in all the way. She's tight and slick, and I pound into her. I'm not gentle. My only thought is to reach my orgasm. I let out a growl when I see her watching me go in and out of her slick, tight cunt.

"I'm going to flip us, and you're going to ride me."

I keep us joined as I roll onto my back, and my cock stays in as far as it can go. She rolls her hips, but it's not fast enough, so I grab them and move her faster.

She moans—she must like this position—but this isn't about her, so I stop moving her hips and say, "On your knees."

She opens her eyes, and I can see desire there. "I'm so close, please."

"On your knees," I say with a growl.

She isn't happy about it, but she dismounts and goes to her knees.

"Move, so you're near the edge of the bed," I say. My balls are screaming at me. While she shuffles back, I stand, and when she reaches the edge, I thrust inside her. She cries out, and I keep pounding into her, faster and faster. I grip her hips and admire her ass as I do it.

The orgasm hits me, and I hold her against my cock as I explode. I ride the wave, and when it subsides, I say, "On your back and spread your legs." I wait until she's in position, and then I say, "Grip your knees." She is completely open to me, and I let my hand cup her core as I slowly move my fingers, finding her sweet spot. She grinds against my hand, so I stop.

"Please," she begs.

"Will you stay the night?"

"Yes," she whispers.

"Will you do as you're told?" I rub her sweet spot again.

She moans, "Oh, yes."

I bend down between her legs and suck on her clit. She gasps and grabs my head. I use my tongue on her and push two fingers inside her. She grinds into my face, and her moans become louder. Then she stops moving. I continue to use my fingers and tongue at an increased speed as she shivers all over, and she chants, "That's it, that's it, that's it!"

I feel her spasm around my fingers as her orgasm hits. I continue to work her until she pulls me away. I wipe my face on the bed and make my way up her body, covering hers with my own. I kiss her, our tongues entwine, and I frame her face with my hands.

"Thank you," I say, and truly mean it.

"For what?" she says.

"For trusting me not to hurt you. For letting me use your body and for agreeing to my terms." Her face lights up, and she kisses my nose.

"I thought you were going to fuck me and not satisfy me. I think I should be the one thanking you." I chuckle at her, and she traces patterns on my back with her fingertips.

"I think we need to shower. Then fuck some more, eat, and then start all over again," I say as I roll off of her and stand up. I walk toward the bathroom, then stop at the door and look at her. She's up on one elbow as she stares at my body. "What?"

"How many tattoos do you have?"

"A lot. You can count them all if you like. Now, my little dove, get your ass into the shower. You scrub my back, and I'll scrub yours." I grin at her and walk into the bathroom.

CHAPTER 38

DANE

I watch my woman wheel my sister away. I have no idea how I'm supposed to fix my relationship with Emily. She thinks I abandoned her and walked away from her. I was fifteen—I was a child myself. I went back when I was nineteen. I waited until my father left for work, and then I went and knocked on the door.

I can remember standing there and being nervous. I was a prospect then, but I had regular work at the garage and an income. My mother opened the door, and she had the biggest grin on her face. I don't know what I was expecting, but it wasn't happiness.

"Dane?" She stepped out into the yard and

looked around.

"Don't worry. I waited till he left before I knocked on the door."

She closed the front door and took two steps away from it. "What are you doing here, Dane?"

"I have a job, and I live in a really nice town. You'd be safe."

"You need to leave, Dane. We are safe, and we're happy. He's changed."

"He's changed?" I asked her, disbelief in my tone.

"He's stopped drinking. He has it under control. You need to leave before Emily sees you."

"But I wanted to see her, to spend some time with you both."

"No, you have to go."

I reached into my pocket and gave her a card with my phone number and address on it. "Take this. If you ever need an escape plan or want to visit me, without him, this is where I am, and this is how to contact me."

"Dane, I need you to promise you won't try to contact Emily or me ever again. He's better, but if he found out you were here, it would be bad for us." I remember her eyes were full of fear.

"I thought you said he'd changed?"

"He has but, sometimes he slips. Right now, he's good. It's good."

"I need to know, Ma, if he ever slips, you'll call

me," I said.

"Yes, I promise. Now, please go."

I remember as I stood there and stared at her, I'd wished she'd come with me. I guess I knew she wouldn't. I walked away, and it was the last time I saw her.

I slowly follow Kat and Emily to the cottage. I can hear Kat chatting with Emily about how nice she thinks the cottages are. I normally only rent out the five cottages in winter, which is peak tourist season here. People come from all over to ski. I charge a premium, and I really don't have to do anything as they're fully self-contained.

When we arrive at the cottage door, I move ahead of them and take the keys off Kat, so they can go straight in. Kat gives me a tight smile, and Emily avoids all eye contact. When they go inside, Kat immediately walks into the kitchen and begins opening cupboards and then the refrigerator.

"Dane, there's no milk, and it looks like the coffee wasn't replenished after the last guests. I'll need to find it at our house. Can you please help Emily into bed and be nice to her?" she asks with more than a hint of sarcasm. "Emily, I'll be back in a minute."

I sigh and look at Emily. "Let's get you into bed."

"It's fine, I can do it myself."

"Em, at least let me wheel you closer to the bed."

She nods. I push her closer and pull the covers

down. I watch as she tentatively tries to stand, putting most of her weight on one leg, and a small smile plays on her lips. "It doesn't hurt as much as I thought it would."

"Could have something to do with the injection Doc Jordan gave you for the pain," I say with a grin. "What about your hands, Em? Are they okay?"

"Yes, a bit scraped and a little burned, but no permanent damage. Doc has put an ointment on them to help with infection, and he's given me some codeine tablets to help with the pain. He says it's only second-degree burns, and I was lucky. The burns were my fault."

"None of this was your fault." She avoids my eyes, and I try to imagine what she has gone through. She awkwardly moves onto the bed, and I move the wheelchair out of the way, then pull up the covers. The cottages normally have the bed raised up a few steps so the occupants can see a view of the mountains and valleys. Obviously, this one doesn't, so we made one entire wall out of glass. They get an awesome view from anywhere inside. I walk over and pull the sheer curtain across to give her some privacy. This cottage is positioned away from the others, and you'd have to be a mountain goat to see in it. Walking into the dining area, I grab a chair and sit down next to her bed.

"There are many things I need to talk to you about, but I know you have questions. Ask me anything, Emily, and I'll tell you the truth. My only condition is you repeat what I tell you to no one. If you can't do that, then we can't have this conversation." I have done many things in my life, but not all of them have been legal, and not everyone knows everything about me. I'm trusting her to keep my secrets. I'll never go back to prison.

"Why did you leave me? Why did you never come back?" Her voice is raised, and I feel as if she's on the verge of tears.

I rub a hand over my face and sigh. "Dad threw me out when I was fifteen. I begged Ma, Emily, to choose me and you and to throw him out." I meet her eyes and continue, "But she chose him, Em." She shakes her head. "Tell me what you were told."

"Dad said you stole a car and fell in with a bad crowd, the Savage Angels. He said he asked you to come home, and you told him you never wanted to see us again. You didn't even come to Ma's funeral." She sounds hurt and angry. I don't know how I'm going to convince her, her whole life has been a lie.

"After Dad threw me out and Ma turned her back on me, I hitched a ride and kept going. One night, I was walking past a garage, and I could see a group of men around a bike, revving it. I could tell by listening to it, the engine was slightly misfiring. I walked in and said I could fix it. They all laughed, but the guy who owned it let me play with it. That was how I met the Savage Angels."

"You hitched by yourself? Weren't you scared?"

"I was scared of everything." I chuckle at her. "But I learned very quickly not to show fear. The old saying 'fake it till you make it' holds merit. Outwardly, I looked like I knew what I was doing, but I didn't. I was lucky I fell into the club. Then, one night I stupidly got into a car that was stolen, and when we were caught, I wasn't fast enough to run away. I rang Dad when I was arrested, and he hung up on me. The Judge threw me into a juvenile facility until I turned eighteen. I had no one, but while I was incarcerated, the guy whose bike I fixed, Roy, came to visit me. He wore his colors." I point at Jonas' jacket that she still wears. "The other prisoners left me alone after that. I was unofficially a Savage Angel, and everyone knows you don't fuck with them. When I got out, Roy was there to pick me up."

"You rang Dad, and he hung up on you? Really?" she asks, and I nod at her.

"I like to think Ma didn't know, but she probably did." I stand up and pace. "I went back for you when I was nineteen. I'd been working here in the garage. The club owns it. I had a steady income and came to get you both, but Ma told me he had stopped drinking, and you were both happy and safe. I left her my number and told her if she ever needed me, all she had to do was call." I stop pacing and look at her. "In a way, it was a good thing for me. I had no ties, so I went up through the ranks of the MC really quickly. If I had enemies, I had no family or loved ones for them to hurt me with. The MC was... is my family." A tear falls down her cheek, but she quickly wipes it away. "But, Em, there's room here for you, too. I always thought you'd find me, especially when you went away to college. Why, Em?"

"She never told me you came to visit. And he had many relapses." She looks down at her hands. "When he'd come home from work, Ma would sort of hold her breath—"

"And she'd ask you to stay in your room until she called you for dinner. If she never called, you knew he was drunk." She lifts her eyes to mine and nods her head, and more tears run down her cheeks. I sigh, walk into the bathroom, and grab the tissues. "He never changed, did he?"

She shakes her head, confirming what I already knew, and holds the tissues to her eyes. "All these years, I thought you abandoned me. Why didn't you come to her funeral?"

"I was there, Em. I didn't make myself known to you or Dad. You stood next to him, and he had his arm around you while you cried. You came home from college, stayed for a week, and then you went back. Why didn't you stay away, Em? Why'd you go back to him?"

"There was no one else. What was I supposed to do, Dane? He was lost without her. He started drinking, he was close to losing his job, and he was behind in all of his bills. He needed me. I thought I'd stay till the end of the year and go back, but it became clear he would not cope without someone there full-time." She sounds angry now, her voice hard and resigned.

"How long before he started to hit you?" I ask and watch as she averts her eyes.

"I spent most of my time in my room, barricaded in. He was... unpredictable when he was drunk."

"Did he ever..." I pause and wait for her eyes to come back to mine, "... touch you, Em?" I whisper as I hold my breath. If he did that to her, if he hurt her like that, how could she ever forgive me?

"No, Dane. Ma always made sure I was safe. She always kept him away from me," she whispers too.

I let out the breath I was holding, then I sit down and reach for her hand. "I didn't know, Em, I would never have left you if I'd known, I swear." Now I have to ask her a harder question, and I don't know how she'll react. "Emily, did Johnnie rape you?" I ask.

"Johnnie?" She looks puzzled.

"The man who kidnapped you. The one who took you to the cabin."

"He was going to. He put..." I watch as she gulps in air, "... he put his hands... everywhere. Then he got a phone call, and I escaped."

I grip her hand tighter, and move, so I sit on the

side of the bed. "You escaped? You were out in the woods overnight?"

She nods. "I spent a lot of nights at home locked in my room watching TV. I've watched every survival show there is, so I wasn't frightened. Well, I was worried I was going to die from dehydration, but I found shelter, though, and built a fire."

I laugh, and she looks shocked. "You found shelter, built a fire, and I'm told when they found you, you had a spear, and you did all this naked? But all you were worried about was dying from dehydration after only one night?" I know my laughter is from relief that Johnnie didn't have a chance to do anything more to her. Slowly, a smile spreads across her face, and then she laughs, too.

When we both stop, she says, "It wasn't a spear, it was a stake." Then I laugh all over again. She waits until I'm under control. "Dane, I don't want this to go to court. Maggie said you have ways of making sure that doesn't happen. I don't want everyone knowing what he did to me. Can you help me?" She sounds desperate, and all the laughter goes out of me.

"Anything for you, Em. Don't give this another thought. Could you help me?" I ask, knowing I'm taking advantage of the situation.

"How could I help you?" She sounds incredulous.

"I'd really like to get to know you. Would you consider staying here until you're all healed? Let me take care of you? Kat is an awesome cook, and she's funny as hell. Please, Em, will you think about it?"

Then Kat comes back through the door with bags of stuff. She takes one look at Emily, and her face clouds over. She drops the bags on the floor and heads toward me, shakes her head, and points a finger at me.

"I thought I told you to be nice to her!" she yells at me.

"Kat—"

"Don't you Kat me, Dane! Look at her!" she yells. I stand up and walk toward her, hoping to calm her down.

Then I hear laughter coming from Emily. Both Kat and I look at her. "I'm sorry," she says between fits of laughter, and then Kat smiles. "Dane is huge, and compared to him, you're little, but he almost looked scared for a second." Emily's laughter fills the room, and Kat laughs as well.

"I wasn't fucking scared," I say with a smile. Both women laugh harder. I put my hands up as though to surrender, and Kat embraces me around my middle. I engulf her in a hug, and I say, "I think you two are ganging up on me, and I'm not fucking sure if I like it."

I look down at Em, and she smiles at me. "Babe, I think you need us to gang up on you. Everyone around you does as they're told. It'll do you good to have a little chaos in your life," replies Kat.

I shake my head in the negative at them both. "Darlin', my life is full of chaos. Trust me, at home, I need peace, quiet, and tranquility."

I kiss her on the mouth, and she pulls away from me. "I'm still mad at you."

Then, she says to Emily, "I have coffee, milk, and I got a couple of Dane's old t-shirts for you to put on. They'll be huge on you but good to sleep in." She bends over, picks up the bags, and walks toward Emily. "Okay, I also got some body wash, perfume, moisturizer, chocolate 'cause every girl needs chocolate, a dressing gown—"

"Did you leave anything in the house?" I ask her with a smirk on my face.

She whirls around to face me with one hand on her hip and is about to let loose when Emily laughs again.

We both look at her. "I think Dane has a point! But you're right, every girl needs chocolate!"

Both women smile at me, and then there's a knock at the door. I open it to find Salvatore on the other side with at least three shopping bags in each hand. I open the door wider, he walks in, and both my girls laugh.

CHAPTER 39

SALVATORE

I walk into the cottage, and I'm greeted with laughter. It's the last thing I expected. I look at Dane, and even he grins.

"What's so funny?" I ask as I look at all of them. Dane shakes his head at me and ushers me inside. "Don't shut the door. Could you help me bring in some more bags?" To my surprise, Emily laughs, and Kat quickly follows her. I look quizzically at Dane, smiling and shaking his head as he walks to the door.

I look back at Emily and say, "Are you all right?"

"I'm fine, Salvatore, I'm fine!" she says as she wipes tears from her eyes. "Go get your bags!" Then more laughter bubbles up out of her. I smile at her, and her laughter stops. "My Lord, you have a beautiful smile." I give her another grin and head outside.

Dane is at the back of my car, pulling out more bags. "Brother, did you buy out all the shops in town?"

He's started to call me brother, which I know in his world is more than a term of endearment. It implies trust and loyalty.

"Most of them are for Emily and only a few for me," I say as I grab a few bags myself. "Have you spoken to her about not filing charges?"

"She spoke to me."

"What do you mean?"

"She asked me if I'd handle it. Apparently, Maggie at the clinic told her I could make it so she didn't have to testify. This is good, it works in our favor."

I have to agree with him, but we still have a problem. "What do we do about the sheriff? He has a reputation of being one who doesn't let things go."

"If Emily goes along with our story, he'll have to let it go. She simply needs to be convincing." He moves back toward the cottage. "I'm thinking you could help her with that," he says over his shoulder.

I close the trunk and follow him back to the cottage. As we go through the door, I can see Kat as she sits on the edge of the bed talking to Emily. Surprisingly, after her ordeal, Emily looks good. I watch as she grabs a tissue, and her face scrunches up slightly. Putting down the bags, I walk to her.

"Are you in pain?" I ask.

"Only when I move," she says.

"Didn't the doctor give you something for the pain?"

"Yes, but he said it would make me sleepy. I don't want to sleep right now," she says and smiles at me. "Are those all my shoes and clothes?"

"Most of them are yours, but a few of the bags are mine. Don't change the subject. If you're in pain, take something," I say sternly.

She looks at Kat. "You should see some of the shoes I got! They are gorgeous!"

Kat claps her hands together and starts going through the bags. I look at Dane, who shrugs and gives me a look of sympathy.

"Emily, I think—" I begin to say.

"No, I don't like it when you call me that. I like it better when you call me amare, and no, I'm not taking anything yet. I will tonight when I need to sleep." Her eyes go to Kat as she unearths a pair of snakeskin heels. "Aren't they to die for?" I look at Dane grinning, and I think I'm fighting a losing battle.

I turn back around to see Kat trying on Emily's shoes. "They fit! Excellent, we can share! You should see some of my boots. Now, baby, they're to die for!"

"Kat, darlin', time to go," says Dane, trying to give

us some privacy.

"But I haven't gone through all her shoes!" says Kat, sounding like a spoiled child.

"Kat, could you come back later? I need to talk to Sal," says Emily.

"Oh, okay, I'll come back later. Why don't you both come up to the house for dinner later? Dave, my manager, and Truth, the guitarist from my band, are here. We could all do dinner together."

"I'd like that very much."

"Excellent! Anything you don't like to eat?" asks Kat.

"Hmm... I like everything really, but vegetables are my favorite. I don't want to be a pain, but I haven't eaten anything all day. Is there more than chocolate in those bags?" asks Emily.

I'm angry with myself now. Of course, she hasn't had anything to eat. I should've realized this.

"I'll go back into town and get you something. What would you like?" I ask.

"No, no, no!" says Kat. "I have bread in one of these bags, along with cheese and ham. There are also apples." She rummages through the bags on the floor, then she stops and looks up. "I could cook you something."

Kat Saunders surprises me. She's gone from spoiled child to mother figure in the blink of an eye. Emily looks at me, then back at Kat.

"I like ham and cheese, toasted sandwiches, and

apples are good."

"Okay, Sal, can you help me put all this into the kitchen, and we'll find Emily something to eat. Em, would you like a drink?" she asks and takes control of the situation.

"I'd really like some water if it's okay?" Emily says tentatively.

"Right! Dane! Come with us into the kitchen, and let's get Emily something to eat and drink!" Kat bosses everyone around.

I raise my eyebrows at Dane, who does as he's told and walks toward the kitchen. When we arrive there, Kat whispers to me, "Do you think you could make the sandwiches without us? I think Emily feels a little bit overwhelmed. I think she needs you, and we should leave."

I shake my head slightly at her, and I watch as she frowns at me. She's a complete contradiction, and I can now see what Dane sees in her. She has an amazing depth of character I didn't expect.

"Can you show me where everything is? I'm sure I'll manage, but are you sure she wants me here?" I ask.

"Am I sure she wants you here?" She's put her hands on her hips and has her head tilted to the side.

"Men, you're all stupid! Did you not see the way she lit up when you walked into the room? And when you went outside with Dane, she told me how you spoiled her and made her feel like a princess with your generosity. But she said she's going to pay you back, and if you want to make a go of it with her, you'll let her." Then she smiles at me and squeezes my hand. From behind me, Dane clears his throat. She looks around me. "Get Emily some water, and then we're out of here, babe. We have a lot to talk about!"

Surprisingly, Dane does as he's told by this fiery little dynamo. It's interesting to see such a big man being bossed around by such a small woman. She smiles at me.

"I don't know what's going on. Dane says he'll fill me in, but I can tell you, she's vulnerable right now, so treat her right. Now, what do you need to know?"

Kat and Dane return to the main house, and I try to make something as simple as toasted ham and cheese sandwiches. I burn the bread, but overall, it doesn't look too bad.

"Sandwiches are served!" I walk into the room with a dishtowel over one arm, trying to look like a waiter. She smiles at me as I place the dishtowel on her lap, then the plate on top of it. I sit in the chair next to the bed. She sits there and stares at the sandwich. "I'll go into town and get you something from the café. You don't have to eat it, amare," I say, thinking she finds my cooking to be less than great.

"No, it looks fine. My hands are sore, and I'm trying to figure out how to eat it." She gives me a small smile.

I stand and take the plate off her lap and place it on the side table. Sitting on the bed, I grasp her hands in mine. I carefully undo the bandages and inspect her hands. The sides of them have a lot of skin missing, and near the wrists, it's red and blistered. I bend my head and kiss the palms of both her hands.

"I'm so sorry. This was done to you because of me."

"No, it wasn't. This," and she holds up both of her hands, "I did to myself." I frown at her and tilt my head to the side. She points to her hand where the skin is missing. "I did this trying to rub through the rope on a rock, and this..." she points to her burns, "... is where I burned the rope off. Unfortunately, I burned myself as well..." She draws the last word out.

"The man who took you did so to get to me. He thought you were something special to me." Her face falls, and I realize what I have said. "That wasn't what I meant." She avoids my eyes. "Amare, look at me." Slowly her eyes come to me. "We have much to learn about each other." She nods. "I want to know about you. I want you to get to know me, but there are things we'll never be able to talk about because of my work."

"No." She shakes her head. "If we're going to see where this goes, then we have to be honest with each other. The man who took me was going to rape me. He was doing it to get at you, as he thought I was yours. He... he did... things..." Her eyes fill up with tears, and she looks down. "He got a phone call and told the man I was a screamer. I was lucky he left the room, and I escaped before he could do too much to me."

I study her face and see pain flash across it. "Amare, are you saying he didn't rape you?"

She shakes her head. "I woke up tied to a table. I didn't even realize I was naked until he put his hands on my back. He touched me, then he..." she takes in a gulp of air and cradles herself, "... shoved his fingers inside me. I screamed, and he laughed. He was undoing his belt when his phone rang. He went outside, and I got away. I ran and kept going."

I lift her chin. "You were very brave. Nothing like this will ever happen to you again." I wipe the tears from her face and kiss her forehead. "Now, food, you must eat. What if I hold it and you bite it?"

"Let's see if it works. I'm starving," she says. I help her eat her sandwich, and we spend most of the time laughing. She eventually eats all of it and drinks two glasses of water.

"I need to go out for a while, but I'll be back for dinner. You'll be safe here, but I'm worried about your hands. How sore are they?"

"They're throbbing right now."

"Okay, what if you take one tablet now, and I'll wake you for dinner?"

She frowns at me and then looks at her hands, turning them over and inspecting them from every angle. "Will you wrap them back up again for me as well? And yes, I'll take one tablet now."

"Of course, amare, I'll do whatever you ask."

"Whatever I ask?" she says with a sense of playfulness in her voice. "Yes, do you want something else?"

"A kiss." I freeze and move only my eyes to her. "It's okay, I understand. I probably wouldn't want to kiss me either..."

I lightly grasp her face in my hands and move into her. I brush my lips against hers, then deepen the kiss. My tongue pushes past her lips and finds hers. She sighs, and my hands explore her body. I'm lost in her, and I want to devour every inch of her, but then I remember what she has been through, and I abruptly stop.

"I'm so sorry, amare, I didn't mean for it to go that far."

Her eyes are filled with desire, and her lips have gone a deep red. "Don't stop. I want you to take me.

I want you to obliterate what that man did to me. I want you to make me yours and only yours."

"I want to do that, too, but you're injured, and I don't wish to hurt you." I raise both her hands to my lips and kiss them. "I want you to enjoy it as much as I'm going to. I want you, but you have a decision to make. If you wish to take this further, I'd hope you would want more than an affair. I would hope you would want to take this to another level, to be a part of my world and to see if you could fit into my life and if I could fit into yours. I don't want or need another fuck, amare. I want you, but I want more of you than what I think you're offering right now." She nods at me. I begin to wrap her hands, and she winces. "Will you take a painkiller now?"

"Yes, please."

"Yes, please? How much pain are you in? Say, out of ten?" I ask.

"A nine."

"A nine? Amare, you're going to take two painkillers, and if you sleep through the night, Kat and Dane will understand," I say in my most commanding voice.

"Do you think they will mind? I don't want to let anyone down."

"You couldn't do that if you tried, you're remarkable." I stand and go look for her pills.

I hand her two painkillers, and when she has them in her mouth, I hand her a glass of water, which she awkwardly holds up to her lips. I finish wrapping her hands and sit down on the bed.

"I'll stay until you fall asleep. It should only take about half an hour, so let me help you lie down and get comfortable." I watch as she shuffles further down the bed.

Then, she sits up and says, "Kat put some of Dane's t-shirts in one of those bags. Could you find me one to sleep in? It will feel better than this scratchy gown and Jonas' jacket."

I nod and go through the bags and find an old black t-shirt. I put it in front of her, and she smiles.

"Salvatore, I can't undo the gown at the back. Can you help me out of it, please?"

"This isn't a hardship for me, it would be my honor." She leans forward, and I remove the jacket and undo the gown. I stand and pull the bed covers off her, then grab the gown and remove it from her body. She's sitting on the bed, naked, and my cock is hard. Her nipples have hardened, and I reach out and touch her. She gasps as I trail a finger between her breasts. My eyes go to her legs, which are cut and scraped, and I remember what has been done to her. I kiss her on the forehead and grab the t-shirt. She tries to cover herself with her hands.

I grab her hands and say, "Don't cover yourself from me. It's not that I don't want you, but I'm hoping to take much more than half an hour with you, amare. You'll be asleep soon." I look at the t-shirt and say, "How do you want to do this? How do I put this on you without hurting you?"

She smiles. "Hands first, then over my head."

I do as she says. Dane's t-shirt is miles too big for her, but it's softer than the gown. She lies down, and I pull the covers up. "Sleep now. Close your eyes and dream only of me." I smile at her and whisper, "Va tutto bene, amore, sei protetto, lo sei." <*It's all right, love, you are protected, you are safe.*>

"One day, you're going to have to tell me what that means," she says with a chuckle.

"One day."

She closes her eyes, and within twenty minutes, she's asleep. I wait another ten, then I head up to the main house.

CHAPTER 40

BEAR

Darkness is slowly creeping its way across the sky. Those of us who are most trusted—the inner circle—have yet again been called out to the barn. It's Rebel's and my task to bring Fith. No one can really believe he has betrayed us the way he has. I'm standing on the clubhouse porch. I look up and see splashes of orange as night fights its way into the world, but to me, it looks almost like blood seeping away. I'm a tad melodramatic tonight. I sigh and go back into the building and to the room where Fith is being held.

As I enter, he stands but avoids eye contact. I move my gaze to Rebel, who gives me the slightest shake of his head, meaning Fith hasn't uttered a word.

"Fith, you and I have been through a lot together. Before Dane became president, I used to wonder how you would integrate into the club without all the bullshit, without all the mayhem, but you surprised me. You've been loyal to Dane and the club, so why did you do this?"

"She had me by the fucking balls. You have no idea what Ms. Saunders was really like. She had shit on everyone. Well, those she considered a threat, ask Justice Leaverton." I raise my eyebrows at him. "Yeah, that's right, the town mayor isn't as squeaky clean as you think he his."

"Why didn't you say anything after she died, after you got the recording back? You could've said you only recently discovered the gun-running, you could've gotten yourself out."

"You all would've figured out I was in on it."

"All right then, why not shut it down completely?"

"The money." He paces.

"The money?" I repeat his statement. He looks at me, and his eyes are wild as he nods. "Brother, it's not like you've been living large. You still have the same bike, the same everything as far as I can see. So, where's the money?"

"Bear, it was so easy. She had deals with everyone. I really didn't need to do very much except keep it going. At first, I didn't spend the money 'cause I didn't want to be caught. Then, I decided to stockpile it. I have over one point nine million in cash."

Rebel makes a noise, and I stare at him. "One point nine million in cash?" Rebel says with a growl. He stands and pins Fith with a look. "What were you going to do with it? What the fuck were you thinking?"

"I was thinking, brother, I could be done with this fucking life except I couldn't walk away. The MC has been my family. I've looked after it, and I've helped it grow. What the fuck was I going to do, anyway? Lie on the beach? Drink beers in some foreign land and have no fucking friends? I was hoping to stay in town and retire, buy a house, and leave the club. I was hoping you would all vote and let me leave in good standing."

It doesn't happen often, but when one of us retires or leaves the club, we vote. Good standing means you turn in your colors, but you can keep your tattoos and still come to club events and rides. Bad standing means you're ostracized, you turn in your colors, get your tattoos removed or covered, and you're dead to us.

"Where's the money, Fith?" I ask.

He shakes his head. "I'm not stupid, you're going to kill me for my betrayal, and it's the only thing I have left to bargain with. I'm not fucking telling you." He sits back down and folds his arms.

I look at Rebel. "We need to get him out to the

barn. Dane wants us all there."

I glance at Fith. "All of us."

CHAPTER 41

REBEL

"Bear, I need to see the sheriff. We don't want him sniffing about now we're handling this in-house."

"Can you wait for me to see him? Or do you want to head out now?" We have moved outside the room Fith is in and stand in the hallway.

"We'll wait. Go talk to the sheriff." He gives me a tight smile and rubs his face. "The longer we take, the longer I can talk to Fith and try to figure out where the money is."

I nod and turn, then walk outside to find my bike. Tourmaline is a small town. It's the kind of place you can leave your doors open and not worry. I ride up Main Street toward the Sheriff's Office at the other end of town.

I dismount from my bike and walk into the

station. Sheriff Morales is at the back of the room talking to one of his deputies. I do a two-fingered wave, and he does a chin lift. I open the pen and walk toward him.

"Evening, Sheriff," I say.

"Rebel." He turns and walks into his office. I follow and shut the door. "I went into Bettie's tonight to get a bite to eat, and Rosie tells me how Emily went for a hike and got lost in the wild. But amazingly, the Savage Angels found her, and she's safe and sound." He sits and stares at me. I say nothing, and I can feel his anger radiating out of him.

"Curious, though, Mr. Finlay from the hardware store swears he saw the Savage Angels carry a practically naked Emily into Doc's this morning." Again, he waits, and again, I say nothing. "So I spoke to Doc Jordan. Hell, I even questioned Maggie, and they both said the same thing. Emily got lost and hurt herself. When I asked if she was naked, Maggie said she'd burned her clothes because she couldn't find firewood. Now, do you want to tell me the truth? I'll not have you and your MC dishing out justice. We have a system, we have laws, and it's my job to uphold them." His voice is full of anger.

I stand there, not sure what to say to this man. Personally, I like him. He's so much better than the last sheriff. He's good for this town. He's hard but fair, but we have lived and supported this town for a very long time, and we'll not be told what to do.

"Sheriff Morales, it sounds to me as if you have it all figured out. We will, of course, bring Emily to you tomorrow so she can verify what has happened," I say.

"Tell me, the footage we both looked at where it looked like Johnnie Vanetti was supporting her as she fainted, what was that all about?" He gives me a tight smile.

"He was asking for directions, that's all," I say.

"Right." He stands and takes a step toward me. "You tell your president I'll be watching. You tell him I don't like this, and I'll be paying more attention to you all in the future. Do you understand?"

"I'll tell him, Sheriff." I nod and open the door.

As I step through it, he says, "Remember to bring Emily to me tomorrow." I nod respectfully at him before I make my way back to my bike.

CHAPTER 42

DANE

I see Salvatore as he walks toward the house. Kat is upstairs making sure Dave and Truth are okay. I meet him at the front door.

"Coffee?" He accepts with a nod. I lead the way into the kitchen, and he sits at my dining table.

"She's okay, a little shook up, but she's going to be fine," says Sal.

I'm pouring two cups of coffee from the machine when Dave walks into the room.

"Dane, could you please pour me a cup?" he asks. He turns, looks at Sal, holds out his hand, and says, "Dave Lawrence."

Sal stands, grabs his hand, and says, "Salvatore Agostino." They shake, and then Dave swipes a cup of coffee and sits opposite Sal.

"So, tell me, Dane, what have you found out about Christina Saunders?" He looks tired.

"Before we start, Dave, does Kat know anything about her mother?" I ask.

He chuckles and says, "Yes, Kat knows her mother loved her and left her a beautiful home. She has no idea what that woman was really like." He sighs and stares at Sal. "How do you fit into all of this?"

Sal looks at me. "Is he to be trusted?"

"To a point."

He nods and says, "I'm affiliated with the Abruzzi family, and we had a deal with Ms. Saunders."

"Dane, did you ever wonder why Kat or her lawyers never challenged you on the transport business?" asks Dave.

"Kat and I had a conversation about it. She didn't even know it existed until we met. I offered to give it back to her or even pay her something for it, but she said no." I take a seat at the head of the table and pass Sal his coffee.

Dave nods his head. "I didn't want her to have it, my dear boy. I decided if that woman had something to do with it, then I didn't want my princess anywhere near it, and it would appear I was right." Dave is fiercely protective of Kat, and it doesn't surprise me he has kept secrets from her, even if it's about her mother.

"Yes, as it turns out, you were." The coffee tastes

like acid in my mouth as I think about Ms. Saunders, who I thought was my friend. "Dave, do you know anything about her which could be of use to us?"

"She's been in the transport business for a long time. I know she ran her illegal activities either through them or around them. She was smart, Dane, but I was lucky, she slipped up with me. She assumed because I'm in the music industry, I must be around drugs. Apart from the odd bit of fun at parties in my youth..." he pauses and smiles at Sal, "... I never got involved. The bands I manage, I try to keep them away from it. I even write it in as a code of conduct into their contracts. So, when she approached me and showed her true colors, I never trusted her again and tried like hell to keep Kat away from her."

I nod and stare at Sal, whose gaze is riveted on his cup of coffee. "Thanks, Dave."

"Is my girl in any trouble? Can anything blow back on her?"

"No, Dave, she's not involved."

"Dane, are you involved? Because if you are, it means my girl is involved. Tell me how I can help?"

I'm sure in all his years around the music industry, Dave has seen his fair share of shit, but this is slightly above his pay grade.

"Dave, Dane is right. Your girl isn't involved. Nothing will blow back on her," Sal says with no small measure of authority.

"Good. That's all I needed to hear. Now, I need to sleep. Will you both excuse me?" We both nod at him, he stands and walks out of the room. Before he gets too far, he stops and says, "I have friends in many circles. If you need anything, all you have to do is ask." He smiles at us, then leaves.

"Everyone who's important is out at the barn, including your men."

Sal nods at me. "Good. Before we leave, could you ask Kat to check in on Emily? I don't want her to wake up and be afraid. She was in a considerable amount of pain, and I gave her two painkillers. Her hands are the worst."

When I think about what could've happened to her, it makes me angry. Kat walks into the kitchen and puts her arms around me.

"How's Emily?" she asks as she stares at Sal.

"Asleep, she may not wake up for dinner," he says.

"Kat, do you think you could sit with her? We may have to work late, and Sal doesn't want her to wake up and be afraid." My woman is still mad at me. She thinks I disrespected her back at the compound, and I understand why she'd feel that way, but it's not the case. I'm used to being in charge and having my men do as they're told. It's rare for someone to question me.

"Of course, I can. I've got a new book on my kindle, so I can sit and read it while she sleeps."

"Thank you," says Sal.

"Ain't nothin', she's family," says Kat with a grin. "I'll need sustenance, though, so I'm taking chips and chocolate with me. Which means tomorrow, my love, you'll need to come jogging with me, so I can work it all off." She kisses the top of my head and starts opening cupboards.

I look at Sal, who has a smile on his face. "If he won't go jogging with you tomorrow, Kat, come find me. I could use the exercise."

She chuckles and comes back to me with chips and chocolate firmly in her grasp. "I'll hold you to that. Now, the pair of you, do what you need to do and come back to us." She bends, gives me the barest of kisses, then pulls back and stares into my eyes. "Don't be too late." She clutches my face and kisses me thoroughly, puts her forehead to mine, smiles, then heads for the door. She's forgiven me a little bit, but I still have a long way to go.

"Shall we go?" Sal is ready to hit the road, and he's right, we should make a move. It's going to be a long night.

CHAPTER 43

SALVATORE

You have to admire these bikers. They know how to treat those who have wronged them. The barn has new plastic on the floor, and Guido and Johnnie stand on it in the center of the room. My men are also here, and I move toward Tony.

"Boss," he says with a chin lift.

"Tony. Have you had a conversation with them?" I say, motioning toward them.

"They think they'll be able to bargain with the Savage Angels and get out of this alive," says Tony. "Is it a possibility?"

"No. We're all on the same page."

Lorenzo steps forward and grasps my hand. "Can't believe Guido tried to whack you, boss. Tell me he stands on plastic for a reason." The grin on his face widens. He has wanted him dead for a very long time.

"This will not be easy for us. The family can never know, so we must make them believe they have been taken out by a rival family. None of us can ever mention this to anyone. Do you all understand?"

All nod except Tony, who says, "We know, boss. There's no need to remind us. After tonight, we'll all be concerned citizens hoping for Guido's safe return." He makes the sign of the cross, looks at Guido, and smiles.

In a slow, casual manner, Guido walks over to us. "Sal, boys, how are things?"

"We're good. You?"

"This situation with the girl has been resolved. I understand you got her back... intact." His eyes meet mine. He's trying to find a way out. He plays with his pinkie ring, the only sign he's nervous. "So why are we still here?"

"This isn't my doing, Guido. I wasn't the one to take the sister of the president of the Savage Angels. You were. What they do with you is none of my concern."

"I'm higher up in this family, and you—"

"Yes, the family." I smile at him. "Do they know where you are? What you intended to do to me?" I growl at him. His eyes widen for a moment. "We thought not. Who do you think will control your business after you're gone?"

His face goes a deep shade of red, and he yells, "Who the fuck do you think you are? You're nothing in this family compared to me, nothing! I have watched you come up through the ranks..." he gestures to my men, "... pulling these lowlifes with you as you go! You think you have the other family members' respect because of them? They make you look weak." He spits on my shoes.

"No, Guido, I don't care about the respect of the other family members. I care about the respect and loyalty of my men. Unlike yours, they do not break at the first sign of trouble."

His red-suffused face scrunches up into an ugly sneer. "What do you mean by that?"

Tony pushes him away from me and says, "Why don't you ask Johnnie?" A few of my men snicker.

He steps back into me, chest to chest. "I'm asking you." Where once his tone would've given me pause to watch what I was going to say, now, I know he doesn't have family permission, and no one knows where he is. I'm free to speak openly.

Without breaking eye contact with Guido, I hold up a hand to Tony. "Guido, look down. You're standing on plastic. You have no authority here. You were going to take me out and probably a few of my men, but you fucked up, Guido," I say with a growl. "Don Abruzzi didn't give you permission to come here or to go after me the way you have. Tell me, did he even know his business was being affected by the Savage Angels?"

"He's old and looking to retire. Of course, he has no fucking idea. If you were smart, you'd be using this situation to your advantage, you'd be using it to bribe me."

I let out a chuckle. "But I am, Guido. You just told me the old man has no idea. Imagine how impressed he's going to be with me when I advise him of the deal I've struck with the Savage Angels and back pay to him his tribute to the value of five percent. I'm going to be the new golden boy." I place both of my hands on his chest and push. He stumbles and falls to the floor, shock washing across his features. "And Johnnie here was good enough to tell us you phoned Fredo to get a background check on Emily. Now, when I bring her into the family, no one will bat an eye. I'll tell them I followed the correct chain of command. I told you about her, and you called Fredo. Thank you for that," I say with a smirk on my face.

Johnnie helps Guido to his feet, then he says, "You be sure and tell that little cunt I said hello." Then he laughs.

Before I can react to his vile comment, Lorenzo is across the room and has Johnnie by his shirt. Guido grabs Lorenzo around the waist and tries to pry him off. I've taken two steps toward them when Guido whirls back around, gun pointed at my head.

"Golden boy?" he yells. "Let's see if you bleed like the rest of us." He pulls the trigger.

CHAPTER 44

DANE

I walk into the barn. I see Fith on the other side of the room, and I see Sal and Guido standing close together. Sal looks composed, but Guido looks like his face is about to explode. Sal pushes Guido, and he falls. His man, Johnnie, the fucker who took Emily, helps Guido to his feet. Then all hell breaks loose. I didn't hear what Johnnie said, but one of Sal's men goes after him. Then Guido tackles him and gets a gun.

Guido has it pointed at Sal. The whole barn goes quiet, and I hear Guido say, "Golden boy?" He pauses. "Let's see if you bleed like the rest of us."

Sal's number one, Tony, tackles Sal to the ground. Tony is wounded, lying on top of his boss. I'm moving across the barn, headed for Guido. He has his back to me, then he turns. I stop moving, and he points the gun at me.

"How about you, Prez, do you bleed, too?" He looks deranged, and his smile is that of a madman. I glance to my left, and I can see Fith headed for Guido.

"Put the gun down, Lamberti, you aren't getting out of this alive, and killing me won't change that."

He laughs. "No, it won't change it, but I'll have company in Hell."

He pulls the trigger as Fith gets in front of me. Fith's body collides with mine, and he makes a gasping noise as though he has been winded. I clutch his bleeding form and lower it to the floor. Jonas and Judge stride toward Guido. Guns raised and locked on their target, they empty their clips into him. He drops the gun, laughter still coming out of him as his knees give way, and he slumps to the floor. Sal is on his feet, gun in hand. He walks up to Guido, points his gun at his head, and pulls the trigger. Blood, bone, and brain matter splatter everywhere. Sal goes back to his man, Tony, and I look down at Fith.

"It was under control, brother, you didn't need to sacrifice yourself for me," I say as I stare into his eyes.

"I could see Dirt wasn't going to get to you in time. One of my jobs is to protect you. That's all I ever did, Prez. I protected you," he whispers to me.

Dirt is my Sergeant-at-Arms, my right hand, and Fith's correct, he was too far away. "What do you mean, Fith? How did you protect me?" I ask.

Blood is flowing out of his chest, and he shakes. "Loft," he whispers, and then the light seems to go out of his eyes.

Sal stands in front of me, and I look up. He offers his hand as I get to my feet.

"Are you all right?" he asks.

"Yeah, Fith took the bullet for me." I look at his shirt, and there's blood on it. "You hit?"

"No, Tony tackled me and got himself shot in the shoulder. You know a good doctor who won't report us?"

"Is it a through and through?" I ask.

"Yeah."

"Dirt was an army medic. He'll be able to look after him."

"Prez! What do you want to do with this fucker?" yells Jonas.

I turn, and they have Johnnie on his knees. Sal walks toward him. Johnnie looks up at Sal and taunts him with lies.

"She'll always remember me. When you're fucking her, it'll be me she sees. She has a tight little cunt. I finally understand why you like her. I mean, she has no tits, and her ass isn't—"

I watch as Sal points his gun at him, pulls the trigger, and empties his clip to the bastard who dared to fuck with my sister. Johnnie is a bloody mess on the floor. Most of Sal's bullets went into his head, his own mother wouldn't be able to identify him.

Bear makes his way to me and examines me for wounds.

"Bear, I'm not hit. Fith put himself in the firing line. He sacrificed himself to save me."

Bear looks at Fith's still body. "He wouldn't tell me where the money was."

I look around the room and take stock of Sal's and my men. No one else got hurt. I place my finger into my mouth and whistle. All eyes come to me.

"Okay, cleaners, you know who you are. Start doing your job. Anyone with blood on them needs to strip and be hosed down. Take your shoes off, too. Dirt, you need to have a look at Tony and patch him up. Let's get moving, people!" I shout.

I take my clothes off, and a few of the others do the same. "Prez," says Bear.

"Yeah."

"Fith put himself in the way to protect you. Surely, he should get a proper funeral?"

"I see what you're saying, brother, but it's too hard. How would we explain his death?" I ask.

"Doesn't feel right, Prez."

"His name can go on the wall. He'll be honored that way. You know we can't give him a proper funeral. We can't."

He nods and walks away.

Sal comes over to me. He's taken off his clothes, and I can see his muscled body has no small amount of ink.

"Let's get the fuck out of here, yeah?" he says.

"Yeah, brother, let's go home." I walk to the middle of the room and shout. "Those who don't need to be here, get out. Cleaners, you let me know if you need help. I'm out of here." I walk to the barn doors, and most of the men inside follow me. I need to get home to my woman.

CHAPTER 45

KAT

I'm sitting on a chair next to Emily, reading my book, when Salvatore comes through the door. He's wearing a black t-shirt and a pair of jeans. It looks good on him. I've only ever seen him in a suit.

"How is she?" he asks.

"She's only woken up a couple of times, but she's been fine. She asked for you once." I smile at him.

"She asked for me?" He looks surprised.

"Yes." I stand and walk toward him. "She likes you. It's obvious. You'd better do right by her, Salvatore. I don't know what she's been through recently, but I know her childhood wasn't an easy one. Bottom line, Salvatore..." I say as I put my hands on my hips, "... we all come with baggage. If she's the right fit for you, you find room to unpack that baggage or, better yet, leave it behind. I know you've only just met, but don't let anything get in your way." I pause, then I say, "Including her brother." I touch his arm and walk out of the cottage toward my home.

The walk to the main house is a short one. I go over the last few days. It started out with Judge and I shopping in Pearl County. Then, it was cut short, and I had to come back to the compound where I was told to wait in the garage's office. I didn't mind being in there, but I did not like Dane ordering me around the way he did. I think he told Dave and Truth they could come and visit in an effort to please me.

I have a band staying at my home—Dark Ink—and they're recording their first album. Their singer, Dan, has a sublime voice. In my heart, I know they are going to be huge, but they need to be managed the right way, so I introduced them to Dave. As a manager in the music industry, he's the best. He takes care of his clients, and I know he'll take care of them. The only thing I didn't count on was Truth being attracted to Amy, the drummer. I think Dan had a bit of a crush on her, so it could cause some conflict. Then, I get home, and Dane's long-lost sister is here looking like she's been through a whirlwind. One look at her, and I could tell she was close to losing it, and Dane wasn't helping. Now she's asleep in one of the cottages with a very good-looking man who scares me a little.

I open the door to my home and find Dane standing on the other side. He frowns at me, takes two steps toward me, and engulfs me in a hug.

"Dane!" I yell.

"I'm sorry, darlin', I shouldn't have spoken to you that way, but there were things happening you didn't know about." His voice is soft and gentle.

"I'm tired. I've been reading all afternoon, and now I need to sleep. Come on, you can wash my back."

He doesn't let me go, but he leans back and says, "Wash your back as in we're taking a shower?"

"As in I'm taking a shower, and you're going to wash my back."

He picks me up and throws me over his shoulder. "Dane! What are you doing?"

"Just in case, I'm carrying you up those stairs and into our room before you change your mind."

I laugh as he holds me, and I'm reminded of my first night here when he carried me to my room. By the time we get upstairs, my core is tingling.

He puts me down on the tiles in our private bathroom. "What do you want me to do?" he asks with a smirk on his face. I have no doubt he knows what he's doing to me.

"Take off your clothes," I say without a smile.

He raises one eyebrow but does as he's told. I

slip off my shoes while he undresses.

"Now what?" he says.

"Remove my clothing."

He smiles. "Arms up." I raise my arms above my head. He grabs the hem of my shirt and pulls it up over my head, brushing my nipples as he does. I gasp. He throws the t-shirt on the floor. "And now?"

"Take off my jeans, then my bra, and lastly my panties," I say, slightly rushing my words.

He drops to his knees and undoes my jeans. He pulls them down, and when he gets them to my knees, he blows on my skin and pushes his face into my crotch. I can feel his tongue on me, so I grip his head and grind into him. I feel his hands pulling my jeans down further. He pulls away from me and quickly takes the rest of my clothing off.

His cock is erect as he picks me up, puts me on the vanity, and spreads my legs, and I say, "No."

"No?" he asks quizzically.

"On your knees."

He drops and looks up at me. "Anything for you, darlin'."

I put my legs on his shoulders and grab his head with my hands. "I need you to put your mouth on me. I need your tongue to work its magic, and when I'm finished, we'll talk about what you want."

He licks my slit, I gasp, and then his tongue works my sweet spot. I can feel my orgasm building. He inserts a finger into me, pushing me over the edge, and I grind into his face as my orgasm washes over me. I use him until the wave of ecstasy subsides, then I push him away.

He stands, spreads my legs, and has the tip of his cock at my entrance when I say, "No." He pushes himself a little further in. "I said, no," I repeat more firmly.

He pulls away and puts his forehead to mine. "Darlin', you're killing me. My cock wants to go home. Let me in, let me come home."

"I need a shower. Let's have a shower," I say with a smile. He groans, then licks and sucks on my neck, and I can feel his erection on my stomach. "Dane, shower."

He moves away from me and turns on the shower. I hop off the vanity and grab the soap to lather up my hands and place them on his back. I work my way down his gorgeous angel tattoo to his butt and cup each cheek in my hands.

"Turn around." He does as he's told, then puts his back to the wall.

I lather my hands up again and start at his shoulders, slowly making my way down to his cock. I grab it in my hands and pump it. He closes his eyes, and I drop to my knees and lightly run my tongue over the tip.

"Fuck!" he says as he grips my head and pushes himself further into my mouth. I suck and lick as he moves me faster and faster, his rhythm increasing.

Then I stop, stand, and take a step back. "Please, darlin', I need you. I need you now." He sounds desperate.

"I need a shower, and you need to wash me," I say, moving under the spray of the shower.

He grabs the soap and lathers it up. His eyes are full of desire. His hands move everywhere. I turn and bend over, place my hands on the wall, and spread my legs. His hands are on my ass, and his fingers lightly brush my pussy. I gasp and grind into him.

"Please, darlin', let me fuck you."

I can feel his tip pushing against my entrance. I push back, taking him into me, and then I stand up and back away from him and the spray of the shower. I smile as I look at his face. His desire is exuding from him. He closes the gap between us, picks me up, and carries me to the bed. He throws me on it, and I try to crawl away from him, but he grabs my ankles and pulls me back.

I'm on my hands and knees, and he has his cock positioned at my entrance.

"Let me fuck you." He sounds raw and at the end of his tether.

Again, I push against him, taking him into me, but this time he grabs my hips and holds on. He slams into me over and over again. I use one of my hands on myself, and I'm almost ready to orgasm again.

"Now, darlin', come for me now!"

My orgasm hits as he keeps pounding into me, harder and faster than ever before. He buries himself into me up to the hilt. "Jesus Christ, Kat!"

We stay connected, both breathing heavily. His fingers trace lines on my back. I slowly pull away from him, and he groans. I fall on the bed, and he covers me with his body, kissing me everywhere.

"I love you, Kat. You're the only woman I've ever said that to. I never even said it to my own mother."

"I love you, too, babe. But if you don't get off me, I think I might suffocate."

He chuckles and repositions himself to my side. "I really am sorry about today. Do you forgive me?"

"I'll forgive you if you change these wet sheets, go jogging with me tomorrow, and make me breakfast."

He chuckles. "I think I can do that."

CHAPTER 46

SALVATORE

I wake up, and I'm naked, cuddling a woman. I push my erection into her, seeking her pussy. When I realize where I am and who I'm with, I roll away, but she comes with me. In her sleep, she reaches for me, and her bandaged hands work their way down my body to my eager cock. She rolls, so she's on top of me.

Emily straddles me and puts my cock into her dripping cunt. She is tight and slick and rolls her hips. I move her faster and faster and feel her pussy constrict around my cock. She makes this delightful noise as she comes and whispers my name. I roll us and kneel between her legs as I grab her and impale her on my cock. I move faster and faster and feel her pussy spasm again, and this drives me to my own orgasm.

I fall on her, putting most of my weight on my arms. Her face is flushed with desire, and I don't think I've seen a more beautiful sight. I kiss her nose and eyelids.

"That was a nice way to wake up. Can we do it again?" she asks.

I chuckle. "Yes, amare, whenever you like. But did I hurt you?"

Her eyes flutter open, and she looks at me. "My hands and foot hurt, but I feel wonderful."

"Good." I kiss her mouth, then roll off her and head toward the bathroom. I do what I need to do, then I go back to her. I can tell something is wrong from the look on her face. "Amare?"

She looks at my cock, then her eyes find mine. "We didn't use a condom." She looks panic-stricken.

"No, we didn't. Is there a problem?"

"I'm not on the pill. I'm so sorry. I don't do things like this. I'm such an idiot."

"What do you mean you don't do things like this?" I ask.

"I don't sleep with men I hardly know... I don't—"

"Men you hardly know? Amare, I think you know me. I have been more honest with you than any other female I have ever met." I sit down on the chair next to the bed.

She blushes and pulls the sheet up to her chin. "I

don't want you to think the worst of me." She pulls the sheet over her head and says, "What if I'm pregnant?"

"So, what if you are? You're mine now. Nothing will get in the way of that. Not even a baby." I'm surprised at what I've said, and yet I know it's true.

She pulls the sheet down, and I crawl toward her on the bed. "Really?"

"Really."

I crush her mouth with mine and reinforce my commitment to her. She opens her mouth, and my tongue duels with hers. I pull down the sheet, and my hand moves up under her t-shirt, and I tweak her nipple. She arches into me.

I roll off her and growl, "Take off the t-shirt."

She immediately sits up and tries to pull it over her head, but the movement causes her to wince. Lightly, I grip her wrists and shake my head. Her eyes widen as I slowly trail my fingers down her torso, then grab the material by its hem and pull it over her head. This exposes her small, perfectly shaped breasts. I bend down and suck on her nipple, she moans and grabs my head. My hand goes between her legs, and as I push my fingers inside of her, she freezes. I stop and look at her face. She looks panicked.

I move off her and say, "Amare? Did I hurt you?" She's moving her head from side to side as a single tear rolls down her face and into her hair. "Talk to me, Emily. Tell me what's in that pretty little head of yours."

"The man who took me... I suddenly felt like—"

"No, amare. When we're in bed together, there's no one else. It's only you and me. I'll not have him in our bed. I will help you through this. I will be gentle, and you can tell me anything, but he'll never enter our bed. Do you understand?" She nods at me. "Do you want to make love again, amare? Or would you prefer I stop?"

"I need you to make him go away. I need you to help me. Please make love to me, but for now, could you not use your hands or fingers down there?" she asks tentatively.

"Down there?" I say with a chuckle. A blush moves up her face, and she nods. "I think I can do other things," I say with a smile. I stand and look at her, my cock is ready to go again. "I'll be back in a moment." I go into the bathroom and grab a washcloth, put it under warm running water, and wring it out. I go back into the bedroom to find she has pulled the sheet back over her body.

"Uncover yourself, amare." She moves the sheet to one side, exposing her delicate frame. "Do you trust me, amare?" She nods her head. I move to the end of the bed and kneel on it. "Spread your legs for me as far as you can."

She does as she's told but averts her eyes from mine. I place the warm washcloth on her core and wipe her clean. When I'm finished, I throw it on the floor. I look up at her, and she's staring at the ceiling.

"Look at me." Her eyes find mine. "Don't look away." She nods, and I move down between her legs. I kiss her inner thigh, and then I lick all the way up to her pussy. I suck on her clit, and she moans, then closes her eyes. I stop and sit up. I stare at her and wait for her to look at me.

"I told you not to look away. You closed your eyes."

"I'm sorry, it won't happen again," she whispers.

"What would you like me to do?" I ask. She moves to close her legs, and I place my hands on her thighs. "No. Tell me what you want."

"Salvatore, please, I feel uncomfortable."

"All right, I understand but know this... I like to dominate in all things, Emily. I'm going to go down on you, and you're going to watch. When you come, I'm going to fuck your cunt hard and fast, and you are going to like it."

Her eyes widen, and she nods her head.

"I need to know you want me to do that. I need to know you aren't uncomfortable. If you are, we can stop this now."

"I don't want you to stop. I want you to fuck me."

I smile and go back down to taste her delicious cunt. I suck and lick as she grinds into me. She puts her legs on my shoulders and grips the headboard.

Her moans are getting louder, and then she makes her delightful noise and again whispers my name. I grab her legs, push her knees to her sides, and drive into her. Her face is flushed, and she holds my gaze. My thrusts get faster, and she releases the headboard, grabbing her knees, opening herself up to me even more. I silently thank her, bury myself inside her, and orgasm. I continue to move slowly in and out, enjoying the feel of her.

"How was that?" I ask.

She blushes again. "I've never experienced that before."

"What do you mean?"

"I've never had an orgasm before..."

My heart swells, she's obviously made for me. To never have had an orgasm and yet her body responds to mine. Yes, she belongs to me.

"Did you like it?" I ask with a smirk on my face.

"Oh, yes, it felt amazing. I forgot about my hands, my foot, and all the pain."

I frown at her. "How is the pain?"

"Not as bad as yesterday, but my hands are still sore," she admits, concealing nothing from me.

"Let's get you into the shower and get those bandages off, so I can have a closer look." She moves to the edge of the bed, and I bend and pick her up.

"Put me in the wheelchair. You don't have to carry me."

"But I want to. Let me do this for you. Let me take

care of you."

"I think I'd like it if someone took care of me for a while. But what do you get? It doesn't seem very fair."

"I get you."

EPILOGUE

SALVATORE

It's been eight months since I first took my amare. Emily is sitting at my dining table talking to Tony, her rounded belly stretching the thin fabric of her nightgown. He's making her breakfast and fussing over her. Where once I was worried she wouldn't fit into my world, now I wonder how I ever survived it without her. My rings are on her left hand, and as I walk into the room, she smiles. Pregnancy has not dulled her beauty, only enhanced it. She is more beautiful to me now that she's with my child than ever before.

"Hey, handsome, good morning."

Leaning down, I first kiss the top of her head, then her lips.

"Has Tony been taking good care of you?"

Her smile widens. "Always. Sal, you need to talk

to him. Tony won't let me do anything."

"Because you are precious," replies Tony with a flick of his wrist. "Do you want coffee, boss?"

I nod, and he leaves the room to get a fresh pot. Taking both of her hands in mine, I kiss them.

"How do you feel this morning? You were up early."

"I couldn't sleep. I feel like an oversized watermelon."

Placing my hands on her stomach, I rub it gently. "You should have woken me."

"You have work to do today." Emily looks past me to Tony, who's come back into the room. "Tony says you've got an important meeting with Dominic Abruzzi."

I scowl at Tony, frowning at me. "What?"

"You do not need to share everything with Emily."

"She's been up since four o'clock. We talk," Tony replies with a shrug as he leaves the room.

"Don't be upset with him. I grill him endlessly on your life here. Tony takes care of me."

I quirk an eyebrow at her. "*Tony* takes care of you?"

"You know what I mean."

Emily leans forward, and I cup her face, kissing her soft lips.

"I'm not sure I do. I think you need to explain this to me in detail, alone in our room."

Emily giggles and pushes me back. "You want me looking like this?" she asks as she points to her belly.

"I want you *all* the time."

A blush creeps its way up Emily's neck, and she tilts her head to the side.

So adorable.

"I love it when you say things like that. It makes me weak in the knees."

"Good thing you are sitting down then, my amare."

With both hands on the arms of the chair, she pushes herself into a standing position, and I rise with her.

Suddenly, all the color drains out of Emily's face and water splashes on my shoes.

"Oh, my God!" Emily looks down. "I think my water broke."

"Tony!" we both yell.

Emily bursts into tears. "I'm not ready."

Quickly, I place an arm around her. Tony comes running into the room, gun out, looking for the problem. It only takes him a moment to realize what's going on, and he puts his gun away.

"Let's do this," says Tony as he goes to Emily's other side.

"I'm scared."

"Va tutto bene, amore, sei protetto, lo sei." <*It's all right, love, you are protected, you are safe.*>

Emily nods, and we make our way to the car.

"Have you been having contractions?" I ask.

"Maybe? I thought my back was just sore."

Tony drives while I sit in the back with my wife. My fingers entwine with hers. Together, we do the breathing techniques we learned in her Lamaze class.

"You two okay back there?"

"Yes, Tony, we're fine," says Emily.

"Boss, you don't look so good."

"My wife is having my child, and there's nothing I can do but hold her hand. How am I supposed to look?"

Tony shrugs and smiles. He's worried about Emily too, in his own way.

We pull into the ER entrance of the private hospital, and Tony gets out of the car to help me help Emily out. A male nurse comes running out with a wheelchair, and we put Emily in it. She has a death grip on my hand.

"You are not leaving me," Emily growls out.

"First pregnancy?" asks the nurse.

"Yes," replies Tony.

"I am not leaving you. Ever," I state with conviction.

Emily nods vigorously. "You got that right. I've got a set of papers at home which say you belong to me."

"Papers?" asks the nurse as he wheels us

through the hospital toward the elevators.

"She means our wedding certificate."

He chuckles and nods. "How far apart are your contractions?"

"I'm not sure. My water broke." Emily looks around frantically. "Where's Tony?"

"Amare, he probably moved the car."

"He loves you, you know?" pants Emily.

"I know."

The nurse wheels us into a room, and we both help Emily onto the bed. "It's Mr. and Mrs. Agostino, right?"

"Yes," replies Emily. "How did you know that?"

"It's my job to know who the VIPs are, and your driver called ahead." He winks at Emily. "Dr. Beadle will be here in no time."

"Thank you."

Pulling my cell out of my pocket, I dial Tony.

"Yeah, boss?"

"Did you phone the hospital?"

"No, boss. I texted Dr. Beadle with a 911. She knows it means we're ready to deliver a baby."

"We are on the third floor, room 211." Chuckling, I hang up the cell and sit on the edge of the bed with my wife.

I brush the hair off her face. "You're going to be fine, I'm here." Emily nods. "Just breathe."

Hours later, my amare is exhausted. Our child isn't in a hurry to join us. Tony is pacing in the hallway, worried about Emily. The doctor smiles at me.

"Okay, Emily, I need you to give me one big push. Can you do that?"

Emily nods, her hair is plastered to her forehead with sweat. She grits her teeth together, and her beautiful face goes red as she pushes like never before.

"Good girl. I can see the head. Not long now."

Watching the one you love go through this and not being able to help them is excruciating. If I could take her pain, I would.

"Mr. Agostino, your child is nearly out. Would you like to cut the cord?"

I glance at Emily, who nods and reluctantly lets go of my hand.

"One more push, I promise, and you're done."

Emily bears down, and I watch as a precious child enters the world. It screams, and I'm pleased they have entered the world on a roar and not a whisper. A true Agostino.

"Sal, what is it? Is it a boy or a girl?" asks my beautiful wife.

With tears in my eyes, I smile at her. "You have done well, amare. You have given me a gift so great I can never repay you. I love you and our son."

TO BE CONTINUED

Kathleen Kelly

If you liked this story,
you can continue with book 3:

The Savage Angels MC Series
Motorcycle Club Romance
Savage Stalker Book 1
Savage Fire Book 2
Savage Town Book 3
Savage Lover Book 4
Savage Sacrifice Book 5
Savage Rebel (Novella) Book 6
Savage Lies Book 7
Savage Life Book 8
Savage Christmas (Novella) Book 9

The MacKenny Brothers Series
An MC/Band of Brothers Romance
Spark Book 1
Spark of Vengeance Book 2
Spark of Hope Book 3
Spark of Deception Book 4
Spark of Time Book 5
Spark of Redemption Book 6

Tackling Romance Series
A Sports Romance
Tackling Love Book 1
Tackling Life Book 2

Standalones
Wraith
Cardinal: The Affinity Chronicles Book One
Crude Possession: Crude Souls MC
Snake's Revenge: Gritty Devils MC

ACKNOWLEDGMENTS

To my SL – thank you, baby.

> What we find in a soul mate is not something wild to tame, but something wild to run with.
> ~ Robert Brault

We are going to run wild together for a really long time. xx

To my Street Team, Kelly's Angels, or is it Angles. LOL – Don't think I'll ever live that one down. Thank you! Please know, you all mean a great deal to me. I love reading your posts about your lives or even when you pop up to say hello. When we started this journey, there were less than thirty-five of us, and now we are up over one hundred! Woot! Keep on harassing me and keep on being YOU `cause ladies, you rock!

CONNECT WITH ME ONLINE

Check these links for more books from
Author Kathleen Kelly

READER GROUP
Want access to fun, prizes and sneak peeks?
Join my Facebook Reader Group.
https://bit.ly/32X17pv

NEWSLETTER
Want to see what's next?
Sign up for my Newsletter.
https://www.subscribepage.com/kathleenkellyauthor

BOOKBUB
Connect with me on Bookbub.
https://www.bookbub.com/authors/kathleen-kelly

Kathleen Kelly

GOODREADS
Add my books to your TBR list
on my Goodreads profile.
http://bit.ly/1xsOGxk

AMAZON
Buy my books from my Amazon profile.
https://amzn.to/2JCUT6q

WEBSITE
https://kathleenkellyauthor.com/

TWITTER
https://twitter.com/kkellyauthor

INSTAGRAM
https://instagram.com/kathleenkellyauthor

EMAIL
kathleenkellyauthor@gmail.com

FACEBOOK
https://bit.ly/36jlaQV

ABOUT THE AUTHOR

Kathleen Kelly was born in Penrith, NSW, Australia. When she was four, her family moved to Brisbane, QLD, Australia. Although born in NSW, she considers herself a QUEENSLANDER!

She married her childhood sweetheart, and they live in Toowoomba.

Kathleen enjoys writing contemporary romance novels with a little bit of steam. She draws her inspiration from family, friends, and the people around her. She can often be found in cafes writing and observing the locals.

If you have any questions about her novels or would like to ask Kathleen a question, she can be contacted via e-mail:
kathleenkellyauthor@gmail.com

or she can be found on Facebook. She loves to be contacted by those who love her books.

Printed in Great Britain
by Amazon